ALL DOGS ARE BLUE

ALL DOGS ARE BLUE

Rodrigo de Souza Leão

Translated by
Zoë Perry & Stefan Tobler

Introduced by Deborah Levy

First published in 2013 by
And Other Stories
91 Tadros Court, High Wycombe, Bucks, HP13 7GF

www.andotherstories.org

Copyright © the heirs of Rodrigo de Souza Leão 2008, 2010
English language translation copyright © Zoë Perry & Stefan Tobler 2013
Introduction copyright © Deborah Levy 2013

All rights reserved. No part of this publication may be reproduced,
stored in a retrieval system, or transported in any form by any means
(electronic, mechanical, photocopying, recording or otherwise), without
the prior written permission of the publisher of this book.

The right of Rodrigo de Souza Leão to be identified as Author of *All Dogs
are Blue* (original title *Todos os cachorros são azuis*) has been asserted by
him in accordance with the Copyright, Designs and Patents Act 1988.

ISBN 9781908276209
eBook ISBN 9781908276216

This book is a work of fiction. Names, characters, businesses,
organisations, places and events are either the product of the author's
imagination or are used fictitiously. Any resemblance to actual persons,
living or dead, events or locales is entirely coincidental.

A catalogue record for this book is available from the British Library.

Obra publicada com o apoio do Ministério da Cultura do Brasil /
Fundação Biblioteca Nacional. This work was published with the support
of the Brazilian Ministry of Culture / National Library Foundation.

MINISTÉRIO DA CULTURA
Fundação BIBLIOTECA NACIONAL

For Leonardo Gandolfi, Franklin Alves Dassie,
Silvana Guimarães and Iosif Landau

CONTENTS

INTRODUCTION

'She'd fallen in love with the craziness in me.
Sometimes lunatics are very seductive.'

All Dogs are Blue is a comic modernist novel about being messed up – and then being messed up even more by numbing doses of pharmaceuticals. Rodrigo de Souza Leão is very clear about what has happened to his thirty-six-year-old narrator. He has swallowed 'a chip', and the chip makes him do things he doesn't want to do. Set in a mental asylum in Rio de Janeiro, Souza Leão's autobiographical last novel is about a whole lot of other things too: the drunken street sweepers from the *favelas* who somehow also end up in the asylum; the narrator's teenage years growing up bookish and paranoid; his kindly parents who are pushed to the limits of their empathy and endurance; a blue toy dog which is both childhood companion and the colour of the narrator's medication. It may also refer to the better-known black dog of melancholia – but your everyday black dog is just a mutt, whereas Souza Leão's blue dog is a rare breed.

Rest assured that we are in the hands of the most reliable of narrators, despite his illness – which is diagnosed as belonging to the family of schizophrenias. Whatever, he totally knows the score: 'Why do all crazy people have the same paranoias?' That's a reliably interesting question. Reliable? Doesn't he turn himself into a plant? Yes, he is reliably crazy. But he is also reliably lucid, astute and witty. He doesn't attempt to delude his readers so much as try to get a grip on his own delusions. If he is coshed into silence by the high doses of medication 'bayoneted' into his veins, he is also reliably vocal about the experience – about what it's all for: 'all this to keep a state of order. We're the minority, but at least I say what I want.' He is sad about his situation (it's no joke), yet he is intellectually switched on and reliably spirited.

Souza Leão is a mind-blowing poet; his attitude seems to be something like: Why not flaunt the language(s) that madness has taught me? If I'm tri-lingual and didn't even have to pay a tutor or travel agent to pick up the lingo, that's the pay-off for all this suffering. He was aware that he had to use everything his illness had given him in order to write – and everything it had taken away from him too. To help him get through his day in the asylum, our narrator hallucinates two friends: one is called Rimbaud and, when he's not riding an elephant to Africa, he is onside and loyal; the other is Baudelaire, but he's more of a fair-weather friend and can be unsociable.

In May 1871, aged sixteen, Rimbaud wrote a letter to his teacher, Georges Izambard, explaining his teenage poetic philosophy:

> *I'm now making myself as scummy as I can. Why? I want to be a poet, and I'm working at turning myself into a seer. You won't understand any of this, and I'm almost incapable of explaining it to you. The idea is to reach the unknown by the derangement of all the senses. It involves enormous suffering, but one must be strong and be a born poet. It's really not my fault.* (trans Graham Robb, 2000)

Rodrigo de Souza Leão would have been aware of this letter – it might have helped him figure that the (involuntary) derangement of his own senses was not useless material. His narrator tells us of his own teenage years, in which he sounds a little like Rimbaud: 'I was possessed by a fertile spirit of modern madness, one that has helped twentieth-century poetry many times.'

It's not all about art though. The always-horny narrator often makes his father cry. His mother brings him tuna sandwiches to the hospital but she doesn't want him to come home. If life in an insane asylum is actually very dull, Souza Leão's subtle achievement is that he evokes the dull and deadening days without ever being boring or making them more exotic than they are. Everything that is interesting about the novel can be found in its light, laconic tone. Above all, this is a novel driven by tone. In this sense it reminds me of Houellebecq's first novel, *Extension du domaine de la lutte*, or *Whatever*.

Souza Leão's narrator doesn't know which is more of a nightmare, waking or sleeping – but when he is awake he always gives cigarettes to the lunatic who bangs his head against the wall. He wonders what would happen if the lunatic were a footballer: 'His headers would be unstoppable. After all that banging his head against walls, he'd slam in headers from anywhere. Maybe he'd get called up to play for Brazil.'

The narrator wakes up one day 'wanting to say beautiful things'. He picks a flower in the garden and takes it back to his room. The nurse asks him if he's 'gone gay'. The asylum gardens are full of butterflies. Slums surround the asylum and he can hear music playing day and night. In *All Dogs are Blue*, the lives of the poor and the insane are knotted together. The father figure is knotted together too. From his bed, he can see the Christ statue on the hill. Maybe it's the sun setting, maybe it's the injections, but Christ seems to be always golden. When he kisses his own father's face, he wonders, 'Is it the kiss of Judas? Will I betray my father in my madness?' A feral murderer is admitted to the asylum. He terrifies everyone and shits wherever he likes. Yet this murderer is scared of the fragile shape-shifting narrator (medication has made him fat and bloated) because his voice reminds him of his own father who beat him.

All Dogs are Blue knows that it is telling us about the layers of language at play in both poetry and psychosis. In this sense, the spare, poetic prose won from the original Portuguese in this translation by Stefan Tobler and Zoë Perry is a breathtaking achievement. Thanks to their skill, we hear Souza Leão's multiple associations building, and if we want to, we will find a network of signifiers linking words with other words. Or we can just go with the story and enjoy its exuberance.

•

The first chapter of the novel is ironically titled 'It all went Van Gogh'. Perhaps Leão had read the poet and playwright Antonin Artaud's luminous essay titled 'Van Gogh: the man suicided by society'. Here is what Artaud said about the psychiatry of his generation:

> *In comparison with the lucidity of Van Gogh, which is a dynamic force, psychiatry is no better than a den of apes who are themselves obsessed and persecuted and who possess nothing to mitigate the most appalling states of anguish and human suffocation but a ridiculous terminology,*
>
> > *worthy product of their damaged brains.*
>
> (trans Helen Weaver, 1976)

In this essay, Artaud (who had also spent time in mental institutions) found a startling poetic image to describe Van Gogh's state of mind – and perhaps his own. Artaud believed that the bullet that killed Van Gogh was in his stomach before he shot himself, that it was already there while he was painting black crows smashing against the purple sky of Arles. In other words, Van Gogh was already committed to death before it happened. Artaud's subversive notion of this bending of existential time leads to the kind of sorrow that can be too painful to accept unless the writer is calmly onside with the reader. *All Dogs are Blue* never deals out this sort of sorrow. Life is lived intensely and with gusto at the asylum in Rio. *All Dogs are Blue* kept me curious and it kept me laughing, especially when the evangelicals recruiting patients to the cause leave a leaflet near the narrator's bed: 'My God! Fundamentalists are taking over the world. They're even coming here to recruit the utterly fucked.'

When Souza Leão was completing this book, he deleted words and paragraphs, structured the pages, pasted and copied and redrafted. Like all writers, he read his manuscript through and made decisions. He knew what he had to do to craft this unforgettable novel. His title suggests that we will encounter a stretch of writing in which reality slips and slides, yet always returns to something recognisable. As for the magnificent last line in this most valuable book (but don't look now) – I'm still thinking about it.

Deborah Levy
London 2013

ALL DOGS ARE BLUE

IT ALL WENT VAN GOGH

I swallowed a chip yesterday. I forced myself to talk about the system that surrounds me. There was an electrode on my forehead. I don't know if I swallowed the electrode with the chip. The horses were galloping. Except for the seahorse, who was swimming around in the aquarium.

He has mental problems, you know. Will there be any after-effects? Deep inside this world of mine, in my room darkened by doses of Litrisan, a psychiatrist came and bayoneted some chemical into my left eyebrow. Another, meanwhile, grabbed a lump of flesh, stretching it more and more so that I wouldn't feel the Benzetacil injection.

Benzeta.

Benzeta.

A searing pain in my bum. Everything around me spinning and I'm spinning, too. I pick my nose and wipe the bogey on the table in the corner, far from the darkness in the room. The darkness is clinical. Only the people in white can visit that impure line. They hold me down again. I receive a kiss from my mother. It must be visiting day. I wake up and eat a sliver of guava jelly with the tuna sandwich Mum brought me. I'm listening to a song so loud that I can't get into my thoughts, I'm on the outside, now the cocaine can't get in. The connection's been broken.

Mum's just come and she's off again.

He still thinks he's swallowed a chip.

She says it all started about ten years ago, when I thought I'd swallowed a cricket.

The things I've had to swallow because of you, my son.

My mum stroked my lips and gave me a kiss on the cheek as she said this. For a few seconds I remembered something that had happened the day before. I had wrecked the whole house in a massive rage. I'll never take Haldol again.

You only got like that because you didn't take your Haldol in the first place, says the chip. And I start to say: It's only Tupi in Anhembi. It's only Tupi in Anhembi.[1]

A sword swallower downs a flame all in one gulp. Everybody is swallowing something at this very moment. It's dinnertime. Mum's gone. The music sends me out of myself again.

I go into my room. I pull out my dick and start to have a wank. Funk me, funk me, you're my motor-bike. Funk me, funk me, you're my motorbike. I swallowed a cricket when I was fifteen years old. It was the first time I'd managed to live more intensely with myself. I saved a house from the wicked termites that wanted to destroy it. They were giant termites. I'm sure I saved that house. I'm sure that for a few seconds I was Jesus Christ.

I'm still in the cage. My mouth has been gagged shut. My feet are tied.

The music leaves me and returns, I can't do any harm, except to myself. Everything started with a cricket. There was a cricket that first day. There was also a gene. Not in the same way, but in a different way. I'm swallowing everything, all the time. In the dark corner of my room, where only the rats go. I'm rotten. A pig. Filthy. I'm wild.

The things I've had to swallow because of you, my son.

I look at the newspaper and I can't read any of it. They must have put me on some high dosage. Because I've not even turned forty yet and even close up, I can't read it. I roll up my sleeves and go play snooker with a street cleaner committed for drinking too much on the clock; the asylum's answer to national champion Rui Chapéu. But first, a born-again Christian asks us to form a circle and says someone should pray. No one here knows how to fucking pray. They're all souls with no heaven in sight. I start: Our Father, who art in heaven. At least I know how to pray. The Christian says hallelujah. She takes my hand. I take out my dick and can't play snooker. I go back to my nine-by-twelve cubicle, where they put me to smile bayoneting my veins. Grab the flesh, stretch the flesh, shove another injection in.

It all started when I swallowed a cricket in São João da Barra. I was fifteen years old. I was coming or going. I was always coming or going. I only stopped to fly. That's what it was like when I was fifteen, and how it all started. No woman ever came out of me. Ever. It was always me entering my mother. There she was, pretty as you like, having sex with Dad. And I saw, and it was only 1970. It wasn't traumatic. I used to go around with my blue dog, my cuddly toy. Just because he was blue doesn't mean he was gay. Just blue. Anyway, it's not like I had thoughts on what was feminine or masculine at that age now did I? The truth is I had already started masturbating, and Dad would ask me very delicately to take my hand off my willy. I remember a psychiatrist I went to at that tender age of fifteen. She told me that I was a man because I masturbated, that there was no reason for me to have an identity crisis. I didn't have an identity crisis, because I spent all my time in our sessions chasing after that woman. She went as far as threatening me, telling my dad that if I carried on trying to grab her, I would have to quit analysis. She said that I was too much for her and complained that I wouldn't draw or make anything with the playdough. I pretended I was a dolphin, lying on the couch. My dick went hard and I rubbed and rubbed while the dolphin swam inside me.

Once I turned into a plant for one of our sessions. The woman thought I'd gone catatonic. She got upset. I did the same thing with a girlfriend once and she had the same reaction. I didn't speak or move. As if I'd swallowed a whale. For an hour, the whale that was inside, was outside, and I was stuck inside an insane asylum. Insane asylums are really nice places, with lots of flowers and trees. I didn't stay in a five-star place, but it wasn't a dive either. I saw all sorts of things when Alfonso told me I was going to Paracambi. This is Paracambi.[2]

Mostly, they only wanted you to keep your mouth shut all the time, like no one deserved to hear you say anything noble or important.

What did all those people in white have to do with the fact that I was throwing up blood? They took me to Miguel Couto. They thought I had TB. Miguel

Couto was the hospital where they sent dengue patients. There was an outbreak of dengue in the city. There were a lot of hippos lying around. Some turtles on four wheels. I passed through the doors of the asylum. I wanted to get up and run away. But where would I run to? Who was going to believe I had a chip implanted inside me? There were so many people around that if I said it was like a home game for Flamengo at Maracanã, I wouldn't be exaggerating.

They stuck tubes in me and started suctioning. I was abducted by aliens.

I saw a light shining through my five-year-old body and held on tight to my blue dog. I passed out for a few seconds. Then Fronsky was there.

We'll be back to get you when you're eighteen.

A whole field of stretchers. People walking around with drips in their arms. Tubes coming out of the mouths of real wrecks. It was all Acneton there. They drew blood from my vein. Now I was going to get a chest X-ray. What kind of a problem can a fat guy like me have other than obesity? I should be at a fat camp, not at Miguel Couto with that dengue crisis. A fern sprouted up next to me, like a beanstalk. I climbed the stairs, held up by two doctors as strong and fat as me. There were all these poor people, really poor people: this was Brazil. A total mess. People lying on the floor. People dead on arrival. People dying. A row of bodies with tagged feet. All armed with their charts. And those spotty-faced doctors who don't know much more about biology than I do, making fun of you.

Look at fatface!

What a fatty!

What a whale!

I did a triathlon once and I was one of the first to cross the finish line in my category. Now I'm fat and sleeping like I did on the day of the triathlon. Constantly sedated, my veins pumped full of meds. All this for a song to invade me; all this to keep a state of order. We're the minority, but at least I say what I want.

The good thing about the blue dog was that he didn't grow old or die. The deal was that I'd take care of him, so that he wouldn't grow old. In the year 2000, I'll be thirty-five. I'll be so old it'll barely register. I used to comb his fur. I liked the blue dog's company more than anyone else's. And what if a blue dog really existed? It would be fucking amazing to have one. And if it had a puppy, would it be born blue, too? If it could bark and eat, what would a blue dog eat? Blue food? And if it got ill, would it take blue medicine? A lot of medicines are blue, including Haldol. I take Haldol to be under no illusions that I'll die mad one day, somewhere dirty, without any food. It's the way every madman ends. A feebleminded woman in her seventies, in a uniform, appears in front of me and kisses me on the mouth. I see pink stars. Elephants carrying Rimbaud across Africa. Verlaine screwing his wife, but thinking of Rimbaud. I'm thinking of Nastassja Kinski and her tiny budding breasts. I'm on the dark side and can barely move, just enough to masturbate really slowly. I come and my hand goes all white, covered by the semen. My hand turns into a white glove. I wake up at five in the morning with a nurse giving me the rough edge of his tongue. I don't sleep well. I don't wake up well. I don't know which of the nightmares is worse: waking or sleeping. I come out of the cage. I've been in the cage for a long time. When will they take me out and let me stay with the others? I join the queue for breakfast. It's watered-down coffee and a piece of bread with a single swipe of butter. I pay to be in this place, but that only covers the knife's one-way journey. Today I woke up wanting to say beautiful things. I took advantage of the little time they left me alone outside and picked a flower in the garden. I took the flower to my little room. The nurse made a fuss about the flower. He gave me the rough edge of his tongue again.

Have you gone gay? What the fuck is that? Fat and gay.

I just wanted to see something colourful back here.

I'll communicate your wish to a psychiatrist and he'll talk to you. I'm just a nurse here. I look after you, the sick people. My blue dog didn't have a name. Nothing I like has a name. Everything dangerous has a name. Names aren't given to differentiate people. If they were, no two names would be alike. Names are given to make people alike or to set you apart from the others. He flies. He travels by aircraft. He is my blue dog. Another good thing compared to fur-and-blood dogs is that he doesn't poo or pee in the house. All I have is my blue dog. I hadn't played with him for a long time. Until the time I smashed up everything at home. I hadn't even looked at him for ages. Not brushed his fur. And what if, instead of being a dog, he were a real, live elephant? Imagine the amount of shit that would pile up in my room. I'd sleep in shit. But at least there'd be a stronger shower than the one back home. His trunk would soak me right through. Like the kids' song goes, one tame elephant can annoy a lot of people. Two tame elephants can . . . what if I had two? That would be the best. I'd annoy tons of people. I'd smoke joints inside the elephant and blow smoke out the trunk. Because I'm all those animals. Except for the blue dog. The blue dog is the colour of Haldol. He's my friend.

Do you want to see something more colourful?
Yes.
What do you want to see?
The sun.

Tomorrow we'll go to the beach and play football and eat bugs and drown sand crabs. Let's go to Ibicuí, to some friends' house. They'll be friends for life. I had a friend who got AIDS, but the guy was strong and he dealt with it, and I have to deal with all this shit too.

We only do electroshock therapy under sedation. The patient doesn't feel a thing. Perhaps a few little shocks will make him normal again? Perhaps everything will go back to normal? I live with a ninety-year-old woman. I like her. She craps on everything. She licks fucking everything, too. But I like the old woman. One day she started eating polystyrene and plastic. She got ill and had to go into hospital. Nurse! A piercing scream coming from deep within one of the patients. Why don't they hospitalise women in the same place as men? Would it lead to complete sexual chaos? I don't think lunatics have time to think about sex. You can see some of them just standing there, rubbing themselves. But that happens mostly in the street. I'm here without my blue dog, stripped of who I am. In reality, I'm no one. It's no use shouting for help. Here everyone's being taken some place worse. And hell isn't the worst place.

My father shows up on one of the visiting days. He's the one who put me here, but I don't have any hate in my heart. I like the man. He gives me a kiss.

How are you, son?

I want to get out of the cage.

He says I'll get out when I'm better. I move towards him and kiss him on his face. Is it the kiss of Judas? Will I betray my father in my madness? And what if two men came now and crucified me upside down? Could the cross bear the weight of this lard-arse?

I'd been admitted once before this long stretch, and had stayed in solitary that time, too. My mum lied to me, telling me I'd been in that clinic's better wing. Like hell I had. It was like Carandiru Prison in there. The worst place in the clinic. Where the hopeless cases go. But I thought there was hope. There were only a few people out to get me, and what if those people decided to throw me a party that day? On that day when the rain poured down, the Fearsome Madman was admitted. When the Fearsome Madman was little, he had psychopathic tendencies. He'd already killed a lot of people, so the story went. Fearsome Madman kissed me on the right side of my face and walked around me twice. He said he'd be my friend. That was during my last stay. I don't know if he remembers me.

It was lunchtime and all the lunatics were queuing up when Fearsome Madman showed up. He spat wherever he wanted, pissed wherever he wanted, crapped wherever he wanted, challenged the nurses to fights; the only reason he wasn't our leader is because crazy people are wrapped up in their own paranoia. Lunatics aren't community-minded.

I had one really wild paranoia. A kind of compulsion. Every time they gave me three medicines I had to take a fourth. I'd give them such a hard time about it they'd just hurry up and give me four. If I took three, horrible things might happen.

The Fearsome Madman started to eat everything in sight. He bit off the tip of another lunatic's finger. The nurses reprimanded him. All the nurses were fat. The ones who weren't fat were strong.

I would always give a cigarette to the lunatic who spent lunchtimes banging his head against the wall. Imagine if that freak were a footballer. His headers would be unstoppable. After all that banging his head against walls, he'd slam in headers from anywhere. Maybe he'd get called up to play for Brazil.

He takes a cigarette. Smokes the whole cigarette. Let's see if he stops banging his head against the wall.

I was on so many meds at this point, I'd developed the elastic, bovine drool that writer talks about.[3]

After lunch I counted the stars in the sky and I didn't see any. After lunch I crapped out that awful food in the toilet. There wasn't a single patient who offered a prayer of thanks for that food. Just because a guy's nuts, does he have to eat this crap? A sliver of guava jelly – that was the only good thing. It was the kind of guava jelly that sticks in your teeth. The lunatics ate it. My mum, every time she came to visit me, made me take a shower. I took it where the others did. It was a clean place, that had to be cleaned all the time. Every other minute a lunatic would come in and take a dump on the floor and leave all his shit there. Imagine if one of the lunatics were a pigeon. He'd go around flying and crapping. There wouldn't be a single hat, cap, car windshield or bald spot without shit encrusted on it. But lunatics don't fly, they stay still while they shit. Sometimes they get it all over themselves.

My mum brought me a tuna sandwich and I devoured it like it was fillet steak. I was homesick.

Mum, when will I get out of here? Will I leave here worse off than when I came?

If you go about threatening people, we'll be here much longer. Why are you always in that gloomy corner?

One day my mum would come and the next my dad would come. It seemed like their consciences were weighing on them for having me committed.

I broke the china cabinet.

I broke all the glasses.

But I got all the bad spirits out of the house.

Here comes the gang to give me my injections. They stretch my lard and give me Benzetacil.

Benzeta.

Benzeta.

I want a Benzetacil injection. Penicillin on account of a wound I have on my leg. I need to lose 100 pounds. A nurse said I was actually kind of cute, but that I needed to lose a few pounds. I could be the Casas da Banha mascot – a lard-arse for the lard supermarket – and sing their jingle. *I'll dance the cha-cha-cha. Casas da Banha.*[4] I was a pig. A swine. Filthy. I had no idea what was or wasn't degrading. But one day, for sure, I was going to create something biodegradable; I'd get rid of my impurities and be clean. Clean on the outside. Inside I'd always have those marks that animals leave, bite marks. With bruises on my soul. I'd always be looking for myself and finding pieces here and there. The Fearsome Madman passed by in the background. He was already out of his cubicle.

When are they going to get me out of here, nurse?

The first taste of freedom is leaving the cubicle. The second is walking around the asylum. Freedom itself only happens outside the asylum. But real freedom doesn't exist. Heading for freedom, I always run smack into someone. If there were freedom, the world would be one big madhouse with everyone in it. I could walk out and about with Rimbaud and Baudelaire. Go on holiday to Angra dos Reis.

Rimbaud killed a jaguar that was circling around my body the other day, at night. Another day, during the day, we ate the asylum slop together. Me and Rimbaud. He was admitted for drugs. He limps a little. Must be in his forties. I asked why he wrote so little. He told me he hated writing. What I like is to feel the wind in my hair. There are breezes that are dangerous for a frail guy like Rimbaud, but he's a clever guy, knows how to sidestep misfortunes. Soon he'll be released.

Back to the cubicle and the injections. They don't trust me any more. They only give me medicines by injection. They think I'm going to spit the medicine out or hide it somewhere. Why do these doctors hate me so much? Five come to hold me down. I struggle like a whale. But then I calm down. Then I'm calm. And I almost don't feel it, them stretching my lard so much. I almost don't feel the pain of the injections.

A beautiful rainbow opened up that only I could see, through a far-off window, really far off. That day I cried because I was alone. I cried because I didn't have a job. I cried because I didn't have a wife. I cried because I didn't have kids. I cried because I didn't have a family. I cried because I was thirty-seven years old and living like a teenager.

Why are you crying, fatso? I cry for the fatsos of the world, for those who want to eat an apple pie, a chocolate truffle. But who don't have the money to buy all the treats in the world. Me, I cry because I want to eat you. Oh, you bastard! Eat you roasted. I'd do like the cannibals and eat people. But I'd rather be less crazy and stick to sugar. Chocolate éclairs, napoleons, chocolate-chip ice cream, coconut sweets, peanut brittle. I'd get so fat, I'd blow up like Mr Creosote.

The only time I left the cubicle was at mealtimes. But there was a nurse who didn't take his eyes off us for a second. What if I worked at the asylum? It must be really hard dealing with that clientele, with all kinds of people. With posh guys from Rio's Zona Sul and with street sweepers. With old halfwits and senile Attorney Generals. The insane must be the easiest ones to care for. Every time, I stopped believing in God. A place like the asylum was a sign that God didn't exist. Or that he existed, and didn't care about who was inside that little hell.

I was still a kid and was at the club having fun in the pool when I saw a small child, smaller than me, almost a newborn, drowning. The scene got to me, and it took me a while to think of rescuing the child. I just stood there. Like an idiot. Another kid came along. He was faster, he grabbed the child who was drowning and pulled him out of the pool. They threw a party for the hero. A party that should have been for me. I stayed in the corner. I realised that day that some people are born to be heroes, others are born to be average. I was condemned to be average. I'd never be a superman.

I'd go back to the cubicle. The only good things were the guava jelly and the nurse's pert little bum. Sometimes I go to bed and can't stop thinking about the night nurse. I'd come just putting my body on hers. Just being able to feel her flesh on mine. The first time I had sex was with a boar. They held the animal by its hooves and said *stick it in*. I stuck it fifteen centimetres inside the animal and then they let him go. I came just because the boar jumped up and down. Its arsehole was prickly. It hurt my penis. My penis hurt so much! After a long time the animal tired out. I came six times in a row. I lit a joint, he retreated to the other corner, and I stood there, high as a kite. I did a lot of drugs in my teens. Once, when I drank some mushroom tea, I ended up by our water tanks, having a philosophical chat with myself. The worst of it was that I found answers. I didn't even know there was a higher me. I ventured a few questions about the future and my I told me everything. Except that after the mushroom tea wore off I forgot everything I'd said.

An armed cop came in.

I heard the shots. I paced back and forth. I was flooded with adrenaline at daybreak. The day broke with those shots. Could someone be hurt?

Yesterday, there were shots fired in here, Mum. Tell me what happened. Tell me. You know I'm curious.

If that ever happened, I'd have you taken out of here straight away, son. You're here to get better. To stop destroying Mum's house. That's all.

Actually, they had killed a guy in there. A police officer knifed him. The Fearsome Madman was involved.

Every day before bed I prayed the Hail Mary. Every day I asked God to get me out of there as fast as possible – and that as fast as possible would be the next day. Later, I didn't believe in God or the Hail Mary, but I prayed. Doesn't hurt to pray. Doesn't cost anything to ask. Some Christian, one Sunday, appeared right near my cell and left a little leaflet. I looked at it and read it when the doses weren't high and they let me read, then I ripped up the paper. My God! Fundamentalists are taking over the world. They're even coming here to recruit the utterly fucked. Religion nowadays just fucks with people. I think they knew there were a lot of alcoholics in here. Religion isn't just the opium of the people. But it's what keeps the people happy. It's a sad thing when a nation needs religion to lean on. It's worse than a lunatic who's been cured, but who will always need the support of another person to be happy. Better to be an incurable lunatic.

Fearsome Madman ate his food with his hands. They say that he killed people and everything. I know that on visiting days no one ever came to see Fearsome.

The pigeons flew up into the sky, ready to crap on someone's head or a car windscreen. I remember one time when a mental patient took some ant poison to give to the pigeons. The result was a trail of pigeons on the ground. Dead. All of them.

There was a lunatic there who was a man but who dressed like a woman. He liked banging his head against the wall and was always shaking. There was another who reminded me of my grandmother on my mum's side, always really elegant. Another who had a really strange habit of filling one cup full of coffee and another with milk, and drinking each one without mixing them. That wasn't something a crazy person does. Once I got close to her and she was talking about Heraclitus and Parmenides with a Spanish accent. She was Chilean. I made up a backstory for her in my mind: that she had fought for Allende and lost, like all Chileans. She was politically persecuted. Abused by the government. She was tortured and wound up in a mental asylum in Brazil. She was a sociology professor. Surely she had children who didn't know her whereabouts and who moved around from place to place looking for their mother. Governments do so many things to destroy the lives of those who are a nuisance to them. Being a nuisance seems to be a condition of being a good civil servant. To see the dirty tricks and not do anything, see people losing strength, people with no money losing money, paying high wages to bureaucrats . . .

All of a sudden I heard screams. Desperation. Some patients were hurling halfwits around. They grabbed the halfwits and hurled them up in the air and into a ditch, too. Less-crazy lunatics were leading the event. Yes, that was an event. A kind of ritual.

I didn't stop being paranoid. My chip was still implanted inside me. I'd swallowed a cricket when I was fifteen. And when I was six, I was visited by aliens who were going to come back to get me at my house when I was eighteen. Ten years had already passed and the extraterrestrials hadn't come to get me. Fronsky hadn't come to get me. The chip is for the CIA and the KGB to control me. I'm important, because I can fart without smelling my own odour. I developed a filtering technique. All joking aside, I always felt like I was being followed. I'm always glancing over my shoulder when I walk along the street, and every once in a while I break into a full-on sprint. Once my psychiatrist took the bus with me, just to prove that there was no problem with riding the bus in Rio, in the Zona Sul. That idea went down with a ton of money, plus her watch. The bus was robbed.

They grabbed a patient and hurled her up in the air. The lunatics were hurling around anyone who appeared in front of them. They threw them into a ditch. The person could have got hurt, but the other loonies laughed and wanted more. They queued up to be hurled into the ditch.

Night came and along with it came the worst thing of all: the soundtrack. Our asylum was next to a *favela*. Rio funk played all night long and all day too. Go Lacraia, go Lacraia, go Lacraia! Go Serginho, go Serginho. Sleeping with that rubbish playing . . . blaring!

I thought there was a really strange door in here somewhere, which people never came back out of. They would walk through that door and disappear. I kept an eye out. Two days ago the Chilean woman entered and disappeared.

I'm going to Paracambi. If you don't eat, you'll go to Caju.[5]

I couldn't stand being in the cubicle any more. My joints were killing me. No lunatic deserves this treatment. I know that in my case, it was punishment for wrecking the whole house. It worked like a child's punishment.

Once I had to write out 'I like the maths teacher' 200 times, hating the maths teacher. Now copy and paste on the computer has done away with that punishment.

When the sun came out, it dripped on each employee one by one. The asylum was full. It was overcrowded. It was Sunday, visiting day. There were set hours for daily visits and a set visiting day for everyone, which was Sunday. I still had my chip, which sometimes bothered me physically. I thought about to what extent my chip had derived from the cricket – the one from before. I had moments of lucidity. They were few, but I had them. Sometimes the drugs they used work. But there are people who don't get better, even with the medicine. What good

40

is hospitalisation, then? To gather together human debris.

When the asylum was full, it was time to be quiet. You could get tied to the bed for any little thing. Stuck inside the cubicle and tied up – that was the worst. A lot of alcoholics were constantly being tied up to deal with withdrawal syndrome. Where the clinics really go wrong is in mixing up the types of patients.

I had a craving for my granny's cake. But I didn't have a granny any more, let alone any of her cake. What I did have was a piece of cornmeal fudge, which was utterly tasteless. But which everybody ate in wide-eyed wonder. The asylum food was the kind of food that gets made for two hundred people at a time. Enter the Matrix. It had no seasoning. It was really bad. But it's not right to complain, when there are so many people going hungry and when there were people in the asylum who thought that it was the eighth wonder of the world.

There was no guava jelly today.

I'd been there for ten days. For ten days I'd been eating poorly. At least I'd lose weight. I missed food from home. When there was no guava jelly, there was nothing that I liked. Even if it did stick to your teeth, it was good. It reminded me of my childhood. Reminded me of the North-east. I wanted to eat an apple. I hadn't had an apple for a long time. The only fruit they had there were bananas. I wanted an apple, an avocado. I was dying for an avocado smoothie.

A cockroach came into the cubicle. I had to kill it with my hands. There was no other tool within reach. The cubicles are made for the person inside not to hurt anyone else, but also not to hurt himself. So that I wouldn't hurt myself, there was nothing in the cubicle. We're sometimes tied up at the beginning of our stay. Our treatment varies according to how dangerous we are.

They haven't done lobotomies for ages. Electroshock therapy only gets administered under sedation. There's the movement against mental hospitals. But where do you put all the people with no family, who are lost causes?

I was afraid of the future. Maybe this was it, living with all kinds of people. Sane people, crazy people, cops, street cleaners. I had nothing against the street cleaners. They were very clean and always wanted to clean up. But being locked up all day long, watching everything from afar. It was sad. It started raining, pouring down. I got even sadder. I couldn't remember love. The last time I was loved, she said she didn't love me. She'd fallen in love with the craziness in me. Sometimes lunatics are very seductive. I missed reading a good book on a cold day. On a hot day, too. I wanted to read Henry Miller.

There were lots of slums around the mental hospital. In twenty years everything would be taken over by the *favela*. The slums kept swallowing up the hillside, and there was less and less green space, and more roofs and ramshackle housing. In that cubicle it was always winter. It was always cold. It didn't bother me, I like the cold. You don't have to take off your shirt. No fat guy likes to take off his shirt. Showing off his flab isn't a fat guy's idea of fun.

I hate mirrors. Mirrors are just good for showing how we deteriorate with age. The first thing I broke at home was the mirror. I didn't even care about the seven years of bad luck. Then I went for the booze and, seized with undeniable madness, I started throwing the whisky bottles to the floor, one by one. It turned into a dangerous place. A sea of glass shards. Some things didn't break, like the glass top of the big table in the lounge, which proved to be indestructible. A table decoration was also unbreakable. There were things that melted away at the slightest touch, that self-destructed when I stroked them, and others that remained steadfast. My father came and asked me to stop. I didn't stop. My little niece was screaming. My brother was screaming. My mother was screaming. My sister was screaming. Our cleaning lady was screaming.

No, not that!

Yes, that. I'm breaking it and I'm going to break more. I'm breaking. I'm breaking. Breaking.

The police arrived and handcuffed me.

They took me to Pinel, the public psychiatric hospital.

Why did you break everything?

I broke everything because I'm made of shards and when the shards invite me to, I wreak havoc. Everything was very calm. Except for me. I swallowed a chip. I drank a beer on the street and they slipped a chip into my beer. I swallowed the chip that's making me do all this, even what I don't want to do.

But I could only hurt myself with all those shards, especially walking around barefoot on the shards.

We're going to move you to the Clinic. We're overcrowded.

I don't want to go to the Clinic, or to stay here.

And I started wrecking the doctor's office, until a nurse came with a bayonet.

Why don't you die?

There are so many old people here.

You wait, I'll survive long enough to expose this whole dirty game.

I got close to Jesus. From my cell you could see the Christ statue. They put me there to see if I'd die a little of shame for not believing in God. There were butterflies all around. The asylum was a place full of beautiful flowers, but rotten on the inside. The asylum model had to be changed. But how could my family deal with me wrecking everything? In lucid moments, I ask myself: what could they have done? On the day of the crisis, no one could do anything. And what can you do to avoid a crisis?

You're a lost cause. You're an idiot, you're fat, and vile. You're just saying that because I'm tied up.

Everything went golden. The sky was golden. Christ was golden. The ambulance was golden. The golden nurses were touching me with their golden hands.

Everything went blue. Blue kiskadees, blue roses, blue ballpoint pens, the troglodyte nurses.

Everything went yellow. That was when I saw Rimbaud trying to hang himself with Mayakovsky's necktie, and I wouldn't let him.

Why, Rimbaud? Let them hate us. Let them throw us in a flea-infested old dump. Let life seep in through your pores. Don't kill yourself, brother. If you die, I don't know what will happen to me. I think about you thinking about me. Rimbaud, everything will turn whichever colour you want. You can't see the sea from here. But you're going to get out.

Everything went green like the colour of my brother Bruno's eyes and the colour of the sea. The sea. Rimbaud was happy and decided not to kill himself.

Everything went Van Gogh. The light of things changed.

Finally they gave me some glasses. But with the glasses I could only look inside people.

NOT GOD: GODS

It was like diving. They took me out of the cubicle. Finally. Now I was walking around like an equal among equals. Some people looked at me in fear. Others asked me for a cigarette. If you ever visit an asylum, take cigarettes. Everyone smokes. Just imagine that bunch smoking a spliff, a nice big joint.

I felt as free as a butterfly taking its first flight. I knew it was the first step towards getting out of there.

Rimbaud appeared and showed me some of his new friends . . . Peter Perfect liked to walk around holding hands with Clark Kent. Demolition Man made out with Batman. There was free love in Rimbaud's games with his little men.

Rimbaud, stop playing around with little men.

Fuck you, you don't know how to play. I'm all about playing. I play, play and play.

Rimbaud took the Joker out of his pocket and told me, You have the Joker's smile. I don't know if you're my hallucination, or if I'm yours.

I sucked the air of freedom into my lungs and left Rimbaud talking to himself.

Maybe I didn't walk all that far in the dark night. It was just three kilometres in the pitch black, and what he saw was a black magic ritual. Then he swallowed that cricket. The cricket I swallowed is the same as the chip I have now.

He's mentally ill, schizophrenic. He has delusional disorder, persecutory delusions. No one believes a person with delusional disorder and persecutory delusions. Even if they were actually being persecuted, no one would believe their story.

Rimbaud and his dolls. The Commander is fucking Barbie.

Get out, Rimbaud. I'm not speaking to you until you grow up.

I play, play and play.

I held out my hand for Fearsome Madman to shake. Fearsome acted like he didn't see me. I went after him.

Why won't you shake my hand?

You're Daddy. And Daddy beats me.

So I discovered that I must look like or remind Fearsome of his dad. He was afraid of his dad, therefore he was afraid of me. I was happy. The guy everyone feared was afraid of me. Me, of all people, just quivering jelly.

I picked up one of Rimbaud's figures and rubbed it in his face. Don't you see that this is kids' stuff?

I want to be a kid. I'm Rimbaud.

The Benzetacil cured my erysipelas. They started giving me medication orally. I'd spit it all out. I'd hide it under my tongue, and throw it down the drain.

They put me in a room with two others. Rimbaud, you sleep on the floor. But the other two couldn't stand sleeping with me. I snored a lot. I started smoking again and then stopped. I threw up a lot. So I spent some time alone in a room with three beds.

I've wanted to sleep with my aunt. But I never could. I've wanted to screw my cousin. Cousins are tasty morsels. The most beautiful thing God put on this earth. My aunt was a stunner. She was five foot nine, big thighs and arse. I've never wanted to screw my sister. She's so annoying that I wouldn't even get a hard-on.

A bunch of ants came out of their anthill one by one. They formed a powerful army. They came into my room and took Rimbaud. Ants are more disgusting than cockroaches. Rimbaud kicked and screamed and no one did a thing. I went after the procession.

It looked like a cartoon. I was going deep into the jungle. Rimbaud was stood upright by two witch doctors and when they cut his arm, I gave a Sioux war cry that I learnt from the Daniel Boone films. Everybody ran. It wasn't the first time I'd helped Rimbaud out. He doesn't know how to get out of his messes on his own. I always have to step in and save him. I'm his superhero.

The good thing was that I could spend my days alone in the room. Rimbaud and I spent the afternoons playing poker.

Rimbaud wasn't used to modern stuff. He was a guy from another time. He had to learn everything. He'd never written another poem. But he was a good companion for wasting away the hours and for poker.

After a while a depressed guy came to my room. He slept all day long. He slept with one hand touching the floor. His hand looked like a snake, a cobra that would sometimes rise up and come to attack me and Rimbaud.

You must be wondering if my relationship with Rimbaud was sexual. Even though I knew Rimbaud was in love with me, I didn't really encourage him, so that I wouldn't break the poet's heart. After all,

I was just looking for friendship. Rimbaud behaved himself and never left my side. He was a loyal friend, a squire.

He liked flowers. Sometimes we girded ourselves with flowers. Sometimes we walked around naked. Me fat and him all skinny. We were like Laurel and Hardy.

One day I saved a house from its wicked termites. It was supernatural. The termites were encrusted in everything. I only left termites on the devil's horns. Everywhere else was freed of termites. At fifteen, I already showed powers. I truly emanated transcendental powers. I'd swallowed a cricket that was wriggling around in my lung.

Like hell you swallowed a cricket!

You're crazy. Good heavens, you need treatment.

He's just fine. What he needs is a good beating.

They beat me with a stool.

That was the last time I took a beating, after I arrived in Rio. They beat me out of shame.

Do you think that's manly, thinking a cricket got you? *You're* a talking cricket.

I wasn't friends with Rimbaud yet. If he had been my friend, he wouldn't have let them beat me so much.

I had another friend, Baudelaire, who only came round every once in a while. But with him it was another story. Baudelaire never picked up, not even with me begging and calling him, leaving messages. Moody git. But that afternoon they were both there, Rimbaud and Baudelaire, talking about poetry and modern life. And all of a sudden she walked past me. She came in white, all in white, pretty and smelling of perfume. Porcelain white. I was invaded by the song,

she comes all in white, all wet and dishevelled
how wonderful is my love

Jorge Ben took me by the hand. And I watched the woman in a lab coat walk by. Rimbaud and Baudelaire disappeared. But then Rimbaud came back with a daisy behind his left ear, and danced and danced. I laughed with him and laughed at him. Rimbaud was a lot of fun. Many people must be wondering if it was Rimbaud's fault that I smashed up the whole house. Of course it was Rimbaud who gave me the idea.

Break everything. Show them you're a man.

I didn't become more of a man for smashing up my house. Sometimes that Rimbaud lets me down. I'll go for days without seeing him, but he always comes back.

•

I stopped getting bayoneted. I started oral medication. Oral medication is easy to trick your way out of. I know which drugs I take. I always spit the ones I don't want down the sink. The ideal way to deter that would be effervescent drugs. Of course the feebleminded are totally out of it and take their drugs properly.

Time to watch television. Time for the Addams family to get together. All the nutters would get together to watch the soap opera. A sergeant, a street cleaner, other dimwits and one guy who beats his head against the wall every two minutes.

I've already told that little doctor that he's going to do his head in. He's going to have a serious stroke. I blsjdsomdkm0ooooeeirrrriruuuuruuiirrriiirii.

No one understands what you're saying. Mad fool. I'm going to Paracambi. If you die, you'll go to Caju.

I want to get out of this place, I'm leaving for Pasargadae.[6]

You know Ana? She's going to kill Marcos. Olivier is coming back for Marcos. Pereira is breaking up with Maju. Lina is going to end things with Maciel. Ernesto's going to punch Parado.

It was the TV, talking about soap operas.

I'm samba. I'm Jesus Christ. I'm everything and nothing. I'm a cool kind of crazy. *Epahei, Iansan!*[7] *Ogum bolum ai iê.*

Rimbaud was dancing to the city rubbish collector's rap. He was there detoxing.

See, son. You're here to detox. Your son won't want to see you this way.

I drooled.

I went inside myself, cut myself off. While everyone watched TV, I played solitaire with Rimbaud in the empty room. Rimbaud stared at me. He tried to distract me.

I looked at the horizon. The sky was opening up. Why is the sky so blue here in the asylum? Why are the days bluer?

Nature is so beautiful and reminds me of a cemetery.

The Attorney General came in for the first time on a stretcher and went to a room.

Sir, there are a number of KGB agents surrounding the site.

He's old, seventy-five. Already a bit senile.

My brother came to see me and reminded him of his youngest son, Erbert!

Is that you, Erbert? Come talk to your dad! CIA agents are surrounding the building. We're all being monitored.

Why do all crazy people have the same paranoias? They're always being followed by a secret agent. The CIA is nearly always involved. My own case (swallowing a chip) was only possible thanks to the CIA and the KGB.

The chip had a strange effect inside me and gradually I came to understand how it worked. Rimbaud was the one who helped me with this.

He checked my blood pressure with a machine he himself had invented. They were strange ways to check blood pressure.

He had a medicine that was entirely his own. He was some kind of witch doctor. Rimbaud told me it was him who cured the problem with my leg. And yet Rimbaud was a cripple. When I voiced my doubts, he used to say that his powers were for others and couldn't be used on himself.

The boy stopped, looked at his dad.

Dad, where are you living? Do you live here at home?

My dad was a doctor. Days and nights on end he'd be on duty. After I said that to him, he started doing fewer shifts. My dad was always a good man, very calm and quiet.

I caused a lot of trouble at school. I'd been expelled from four schools. I was sixteen. They warned me that I'd have to go to night school, with adults. My dad cried so hard.

That was the story of my life: making my dad cry.

•

An American guy was committed. The guy had been a combatant in Vietnam.

Motherfucker. Fire in the line zone, he shouted.

Fire, he shouted.

The sergeant soon fell in with the American.

Rimbaud used to do a dance called the Dance of the Blue Pelican. It was one hell of a wiggly dance, using all parts of his body. He learnt it in Africa, he says. But were there pelicans in Africa? He was free to say whatever he wanted. Actually we all are, but whether it's true or not is another matter. The truth can be such a sloppy invention and still convince everyone. You just have to be forceful. Or take advantage of people's natural gullibility.

I've defecated on myself on occasion. I wet the bed on my first day in the asylum so they wouldn't take me away from where I was. This is a life full of abject acts. A life full of fears.

I never eat shit. Nor am I given to macabre rituals. I'm loco-lite, the diet version. Even though my problem with the chip is pretty hardcore.

When I was a little boy, I wanted to be a fireman. I had the outfit, little engine and everything. I had such a happy smile back then. A smile that's gotten grimy over time, like those big family portraits. I was always happy like Rimbaud. Nowadays I think about everything I do and I know when I screw up: when I'm made to swallow a chip and I wreck the whole house. God, I messed things up. How old do you have to be, to be happy? You're only happy in the past. I'm alone in the room. No one's been to visit me for a while. I didn't get locked up because I'd harmed anybody. The only person affected by my behaviour is me.

Liar! Your mother picks up the tab for the things you broke.

All that damn jewellery.

And even your grandmother's china cabinet.

Why did I do it? The guilt won't go away . . . Tear down a door. A rickety door. Why did they call the police? Nowadays it's the police who come to get you. I had a row with the cops, made them understand it was a chip. One of them didn't even know what a chip was.

What he wanted to do was slip the handcuffs on.

I had my first attack at fifteen. At thirty-six I've still got problems. Wonder what the next problem will be? I'm a walking problem.

It rains and I cry. I cry and it rains. The sounds of Rio funk raping my eardrums.

Go Serginho.

I imagine being out of this place. I'd throw a huge party at my house. Rimbaud showed up: Where am I in your thoughts?

You're playing with Baudelaire.

I hate Baudelaire. He acts like an old man. He's very formal. I want to be with you.

Don't tell me you're in love.

I was always distant. When I was a teenager I took the bus by myself from Campos to São João da Barra. I took the wrong bus. Alone. By myself. And so I wound up walking for three hours in the middle of some scrubland. I wasn't allowed to travel because I'd screw up. One time I went to Rio Grande do Sul and slept outside my friend's house. I ended up at the police station, accusing my friend of nothing. The police didn't take me seriously. He's just another nutcase. His poor parents. Get a load of this story, what a pile of crap! You should walk around a bit. Walk over there and back again.

A banana bar. Who wants a banana bar? A banana bar. Who wants a banana bar? Who wants to buy a banana bar?

The sun was a ball of mango ice cream. It was beach weather. And there was everyone burning like sardines in a frying pan. On drips. Dripping with sweat.

I heard a scream from inside. I ran to see. Fearsome was upside down in a corner of his room. Who killed Fearsome Madman? It was you. He was afraid of you. You're going to be crucified. Fearsome had had a heart attack. No one saw. But there was a lunatic who kept saying I was guilty. Detectives – A detectives and B detectives – had gone undercover among us to see who killed Fearsome. I was smart and had already figured out that the cops had infiltrated us.

The days went by and the nights were calm. Everyone slept peacefully. Just me and Rimbaud were awake. Had somebody killed Fearsome? There's a lot of people here. He didn't get along with anyone. He was off his rocker, as Mum would say.

We'll arrive in Cabo Frio today. And be in Búzios two hours from now. They killed a boy in Búzios. They're saying it was your uncle. Your uncle's a poof, but he doesn't mess around with kids. He never laid a hand on any of you.

I was at work and heard my mum tell me to go home. I knew that my grandfather was ill. Grandpa died that day.

Mum, what's death?

Death is a soap opera on Globo, son.

Fearsome went by in a wheelchair. He was so fat, he wouldn't fit on a stretcher.

How could an oaf like that be the Fearsome Madman?

Only Batman could solve that problem.

The Fearsome Madman, who has pestered the people of this town for fifteen years, died today in the city asylum. Some say he was hanged. Others, that he had a heart attack.

Turn off the TV. It's on all day long.

Another terrified scream. They stole some evangelical pamphlets and another thousand dollars. I was starting to distrust my own shadow. Could Rimbaud be involved? He didn't like TV. I'm afraid of Rimbaud. I'm fucking afraid of Rimbaud.

Your uncle's a faggot (hahahaha . . .). Watch it, he might take you up the arse.

Don't say that, it's just going to make things worse for your uncle. This is a small town.

Must have been someone from outside who screwed the little boy.

My uncle was a joker. He liked to drink coffee. He liked to drink free coffee. He would have lunch in *botecos*. Those trashy *botecos* that serve pickled eggs and malt beer. He would eat his food leisurely. Pay for the food. Chat with everyone at the bar. Become friends with the staff. He loved a good joke.

You've got something on your face.

Where?

He would point at the man's face.

Go to the toilet and get yourself cleaned up, young man!

The guy would leave and go to the toilet. Seizing his opportunity, my uncle would drink the guy's coffee and leave. He did that a lot. One day, the fifth time he pulled the scam, the coffee was too hot. He took too long. The guy came back and beat him up. He gave him such a beating that he never tried that dirty trick again.

My uncle had money but he would do it for the adrenaline rush.

A lot of people do things just for the adrenaline rush.

Rimbaud was walking along the wall.

Get down, you fuckwit. Careful.

I went to my room so I wouldn't feel my adrenaline rising. Rimbaud soon came looking for me.

I'm alone. That's how this world is. Where's Baudelaire? He's playing snooker.

It's so sad when your friends are two hallucinations. One that's with me nearly all the time and the other who just shows up every now and then. Get out Rimbaud, you're just a hallucination.

The doctors at the clinic treated people like customers.

You're going to have shocks, but you'll be sedated.

Dad, I'll do anything to get better.

Shocks under sedation don't cause those traditional muscle contractions. It's more like a nervous tic.

Rimbaud appeared and said that everything was going to be all right.

Night came and it was cold that day. Made you feel like building a bonfire in the asylum. A big bonfire. But the B agents were working on the case of Fearsome Madman's death.

Why was Fearsome Madman afraid of you?

Who knows. I had to act like I was crazy. And I did it really well when I wanted to. Don't try to be crazier than you really are.

He must have been afraid of my voice.

There's nothing wrong with your voice. It's not even deep.

But apparently it sounds like his dad's voice.

Insufficient explanation. Did you know Fearsome Madman outside?

That interrogation was fucking rough. I wouldn't harm a fly. Much less kill one.

Talk to Rimbaud. Talk to Baudelaire.

We're going to build a bonfire. Tons of lunatics around here. Are you a lunatic?

I went to bed.

The lunatic with a cobra in his hands wasn't there any more. He'd been released. The room was free. I had a wank while thinking about the hottest nurse. The one that *came all in white*. Then I heard the bell ring for medicine time. The bell echoed shrilly throughout the asylum. The whole gang started to gather.

It had been days since I'd seen Rimbaud. Baudelaire had disappeared, too. It was better being without them.

I missed my room. My blue dog too. I'd never slept away from home, in a friend's house.

At my friend's house I watched Esper on TV.[8] I ate meatballs. I didn't have problems eating. I always ate everything. I slept on the floor.

When my cousin would come over, my grandfather used to say:

Let your cousin sleep in your bed.

I won't.

Your cousin wants you to go work in Brasília.

Only if I get there in a VW Brasília. I have to graduate first.

Then they died in that plane crash.

I didn't kiss the first girl I loved. I went and kissed another girl to learn how, so that I could kiss the one I loved better. The one I loved saw and gave me the boot.

They bought a karaoke machine and put it in the TV lounge. It was one of those where you sing your heart out while the lunatics dance. The sergeant thought he was Frank Sinatra. He sang that old crooner Altemar Dutra. He was awful. My ears aren't potties. The city street sweeper sang that *sertanejo* song 'Boemia'.[9] To each his own.

The B agents were still onto me. They were pestering me with that idea that I'd killed Fearsome.

It was you. You were close. He was afraid of you.

It wasn't me.

Rimbaud appeared, gyrating and singing 'Light My Fire'.

You're the one who killed him. It was you. You killed Fearsome Madman.

I started living with more of that paranoia in my head. Now I didn't even know any more if I *had* been involved in Fearsome's death. Rimbaud said I had.

Breakfast on the table. Toast. Jam. Hot chocolate. Sliced cheese. The table at home, with a new table-cloth on it.

Bread with a single swipe of butter. The table in the asylum.

Three more police officers committed.

My room (I was still alone) is going to get overcrowded.

Three in the morning. I woke up and took a leak. In the dark I saw one cop rubbing on the other. The next day I didn't remember a thing.

Nothing bothers people like karaoke. It's everyone wanting to sing all the time. The halfwit knocked out 'Andança' and 'Festa do Sol'. Why do these karaoke machines come with pre-installed songs that everyone knows how to sing?

Rimbaud screamed in my eardrums: you killed him. I didn't believe my friend. I'd never harm a fly. I treated flies really well. I'd catch them, keep them in plastic bags and release them in other surroundings.

I went to my room. It was empty and full of fireflies. There were so many that I had to turn off the light. They came at me. I went to take a shower. Was there a murderer among us? If so, I could be at risk. I told my dad I was at risk. He talked about my treatment. He said the B Cops had put a ban on anyone leaving. I speculated that that would cause more psychotic episodes among the psychotics. My dad said that if there were a murderer, he'd have to be arrested.

They should have everything settled in a week, son. Hold tight a bit longer.

I'll either leave here dead – or something worse.

I wasn't going to stay there in the shower for an hour. The murderer could sneak up on me, like in *Psycho*.

I don't think the insanity inside me comes from my dad or my mum. But the gene is definitely from my dad's family. My grandmother has a horrible persecution complex. She thinks my dad doesn't like her. Thinks we should pay her rent.

The whole gang queued up to eat meatballs with rice and beans for lunch. It wasn't the choice of food that was the problem, it was how it was made. In large quantities, as if for animals. You couldn't demand nice table manners in that place.

The B Cops are after you.

Me and everyone else in here. But I didn't kill anyone.

I know you didn't. I was with you, said Baudelaire.

You could tell that to Rimbaud.

Lots of elephants walking round in a circle. Each one holding on to the tail of the next.

I no longer knew who to call on to keep from getting smashed against the wall by the B Cops. They had a certain verbal aggressiveness that I didn't like. Maybe it was their tone of voice.

The family wants to know who killed Fearsome Madman.

His family never came to see him. They just dumped him here.

Do you hate your family?

I hate all of them.

As far as I know they come to see you every day. Do you hold something against them?

What does that have to do with Fearsome Madman's death?

We think that only a very stable person could kill Fearsome. Fearsome Madman wasn't just any madman.

•

Night came and I could finally go to my room and enjoy a beach holiday in Porto de Galinhas. I turned up the volume on my Walkman. I tuned the radio to rock and to hell with being here.

Rimbaud showed up as a juggler, with fire torches in his hands. He swivelled his hips with them in his hands. He ate the fire. He breathed out the fire. He was a human dragon. But I was getting better and I knew that Rimbaud was a hallucination who came to pester me. I can't deny that he was pretty entertaining.

I want a JD.

I'm not going to drink.

After the show I gave you, you're not going to give me a Jack Daniel's?

I decided not to answer Rimbaud.

You're not going to talk to me. You can't live without my recognition.

It's true that hallucinations are negative things. But they really could be trained in positive thinking.

Don't do that. It's wrong.

But how can I be so easily led by the hallucinations?

The wind cuts the midday knife. Zarathustra must be walking through the forest. How do you fly without moving? Does a noontime love exist? When she walks by me, I drool.

Daddy came alone today. He said that my brother wanted to come and see me. My brother is sicker than me. I feel sorry for my dad. Shouldering these two burdens. My brother is bipolar. He suffers from being sad. He suffers a lot. My dad studied psychiatry because of him, and then because of me. My dad was a paediatrician. Now he's a psychiatrist.

I would like to have studied at Cambridge. So I could help my sons more.

My dad cried. We all cried.

I've been seeing Rimbaud since I was twenty-three. Baudelaire showed up later.

I couldn't even bear to hear someone say goodnight. If someone said goodnight, they had to repeat it three more times.

My life in the world of colours was hell. I only wore navy-blue trousers and white shirts. I didn't wear black or designer clothes.

The clothes walked around on their own. They walked around the bonfire on their own, like spectres. Some clothes threw themselves into the fire. They were partying it up that night.

Schizophrenics with delusional disorder have no words. They harbour a great hatred for the disease. No one values what they say. I couldn't tell anyone that Rimbaud thought I'd killed Fearsome Madman. Not Baudelaire. He knew I hadn't done anything.

Fronsky was supposed to come get me when I was eighteen and he still hasn't shown up in his flying saucer. They say that seeing flying saucers is crazy. After Haldol very few people see saints or UFOs.

There was a beast roaring in my belly. I asked for food. A snack came and it had cake. It was a cake. All the lunatics queued up. The Attorney General and the drug addict were fighting over the cup of coffee.

I'm going to Paracambi. If you don't eat, you'll go to Caju.

The toilet was fucking filthy. That horrible chill. A night cold enough for snow. Snow fell from the sky. It was California. California gave me a kiss and brought the drugs.

California was the name of the therapist who led a group session once a week. Only the feeble-minded didn't take part. I told the story of Garnizé, who was not only gay, but had a gay son, too. They both had AIDS.

Take your hand off my tits.

Pow! Bang! Crazy Nerd and Silver Alky were going at each other.

Take your hand off my tits. Take your hand off. Take it off.

Pow! Bang! The two were rolling on the floor. Two monster nurses – strong, fat men – came and broke them up. Crazy Nerd was tied to his bed.

They're all watching TV. No one blinks. Every two minutes you hear the sound of a dimwit's head against the wall. He had already made a dent in the wall.

The Brazil match. Please let us watch the match.

You can watch until ten o'clock.

Rimbaud runs by, heading for my room. I'm watching the match. Brazil plays well. Goal.

We went to bed late. Daddy came to sleep at home today. Mummy made an orange cake. It was delicious. Every Friday there's cake.

They held me down and put on the straitjacket.

Now everyone's going to do a drawing. I drew Christ on the cross. Now everyone's going to show their drawings.

I do a drawing of the sky and the sea. It's when the sky meets the sea at infinity.

In mine, there's a hummingbird putting pollen on each star in the night sky.

You and your drawings.

It's how I feel, crucified. In the old days, anyone who was different or who appeared to be a threat was crucified. Nowadays you wind up in places like asylums, which is the best way to not get better.

The B Cops got close to me. They came over like they were buddies.

It's all right, it wasn't you, our apologies. We're nocturnal animals. Images and strange sounds get us going. Here, screams are the means of communication. There's an enigma behind every lunatic.

The man inside the milk carton slapped another man inside a Colorama shampoo bottle. He was a different kind of guy; he liked to go shopping with his mum. I always ended up with a sweet in my hand for good behaviour.

They did the same in the asylum: if everyone behaved themselves, load them up with endorphins, ie guava jelly. How can you miss a place that no one comes from, that people only go to? People only ever go to the asylum.

The Lady of All Screams sits down next to me. No one knows why or for whom she screams. They say she lost a lover and became that way, possessed by the scream. It's a uterine scream. A horrible thing. It destroys our eardrums. She eats her meatloaf slowly, like it was fillet steak. Uses her cutlery with precision. The mistress of her own etiquette. Leaves her guava jelly and screams. With her left hand she picks her nose and wipes a bogey on the table.

Some people there aren't crazy, they're just old, senile, and seem to live in another time. Granny, for example, is always well dressed in a tailored suit. She's a fine lady. She goes around made up, well preserved for her seventy years.

There's not a lot of chit-chat. Idle chin-wagging. Here it all boils down to screams or to *I'm going to Paracambi. If you don't eat, you'll go to Caju.*

What is loneliness? It's living without obsessions. But sometimes in life we have to choose between pounding the tip of a knife or letting ourselves get burned in the fire.

Which is worse?

A man dressed in jelly blew a kiss inside a Coca-Cola bottle.

You shouldn't write about asylum life.

No. Everyone has an asylum nearby. Either your handbag is an asylum, or your home, or even your wallet. Lots of things can be an asylum. I'm not talking about untidiness, I'm talking about real asylums.

Rimbaud showed up dressed like an Apache Indian. He said I was turning into General Custer.

There were lots of flowers around the clinic. It was a nice place. That's why I say asylums are such pretty places that they remind you of cemeteries. Those cemeteries with huge gardens.

Rimbaud liked playing with fire. He lit candles. Baudelaire liked the dark. But he didn't like fighting and he often disappeared when Rimbaud showed up. Rimbaud was my friend all the time. A real wild child.

I'd never met anyone who'd been beaten.

So I went to Disneyland and beat the shit out of Pluto, machine-gunned Mickey Mouse. All because I liked National Kid and the Venusian Incas.[10] Violence is so fascinating, and our lives, so normal. I'm talking about a specific kind of violence. Everything can be violent. Even God.

Not God: gods.

I have rituals. I light one cigarette after another and let them smoke. I let each of the gods smoke their own cigarette. Sometimes I light them all at once.

My gods smoke with me. It's a mess, an orgy of smoke. And Rimbaud dances. Baudelaire runs away. I smile.

What if they were joints? The gods would get totally stoned and turn into devils for life. They'd come in gods and go out demons.

HUMPHREY BOGART VERSUS
CHARLES LAUGHTON

The B Cops decide to leave the asylum. They didn't
come to any conclusions. What is a conclusion? It's
the certainty of having lost your defences. Someone
opens a bottle of Coca-Cola. Someone looks for a
recipe for happiness. Some eel in my hair declares
that electroshock treatment is for getting back to
normal. But do I really want to get my normal back?
I don't know about the cricket and the blue dog.
They're just blue animals. Blue is also the colour of
her eyes. Granny comes and hugs me. She wants to
dance a tango, but I don't know how to dance so
slowly. I dance to a different beat. *Acugêlê banzai!*[11]

I've been to Japan. It was a different kind of place.
Not unlike an asylum. Full of people. Sometimes,
when I think back on Japan, I remember Fearsome
Madman. He was a nice guy. He'd killed six people.

Strangled. Raped. He was a weird guy, but gentle with me. Like I said, he was afraid of my voice when I spoke in a lower, deeper pitch. Fearsome liked playing chess with himself. Who killed Fearsome Madman? It was a mystery that echoed throughout the little silence that existed in a place like that. I want to fill that silence with my voice.

In my voice, a scream.

But Haldol holds me back. It holds back my screams, whispers. I, having hidden tons of pills under my tongue, now take them all, no questions asked. Who knows if they help. I just know that I miss my two friends. Rimbaud appears and tells me he has AIDS. He wants us to become blood brothers. I agree to it and cut my thumb. Baudelaire appears and says he wants to become our blood brother too. Just the idea of dying from something other than the chip (or cricket) makes me happy. To die with Rimbaud and Baudelaire. Nothing could be better. *Acugêlê banzai!*

I've been to China. Saying it like that makes it sound like I've travelled a lot. It was a very pretty place, full of people, bicycles and lots of clouds. The clouds, the clouds. There I was hungry, I was thirsty, I was a foreigner and I was madly in love with those far-away clouds, oh those wonderful clouds! Shapes in the sky. When the day is like that, a sunny day, a day like today, I no longer want to get out of here. I'll sleep in the calm green of 6 mg of Lexotan. Hold on tight to my blue dog and enter into a pact with happiness. Remember China, its bicycles, its blood-red flag and, finally, those incredible clouds in the Chinese sky. I think I'll be happier once I've taken the bloody blood oath. I want to die of anything, anything but of a chip I swallowed. I swallow the pills. One day, I swallowed three. Another day, I swallowed four. I don't really know what I should do to get better. Simply because I'm a pterodactyl in a cage. A raven pecking at the belly of a scarecrow. A man who isn't afraid of the terror of living without fear. Nevermore, no one here is afraid. Not even the Attorney General. He reminds me of a character in a Western or a gangster film. He uses a spoon instead of a knife. The Attorney plays that dangerous game where you stab the gaps between all your fingers with a knife, or in this case, a spoon. We only have spoons here. The old man does it skilfully, as if he'd been practising for a long time. Just for kicks. Letting the winds of adrenaline blow.

Rimbaud appears during gales. The winds that bring him make me wrap up in his scarf. He smokes weed.

Puffs of smoke from Baudelaire's pipe disperse close to me. He tells me that he's a *macumba* priest. He tells me he has powers. He renews my language. I believe him completely. Rimbaud is the storm. Baudelaire is the wind. One takes ether. The other, cocaine.[12] I'm just sad – I'm the guy who finds out that the coloured pills make me fat and stop me, more and more, from spending time with these old friends of mine. What's life without friends? I'm like Emmanuel Bove, who secretly loved the friends he didn't have. I'm friends with my eyes. They only see what I want. I look through my tinted glasses and see everything in black and white. Everything looks like a Bergman film.

Actually, I look a bit like Charles Laughton.

Just for a while, hopefully. Why drink coffee with sugar when you're fat? Everything with lots of sugar. I look at clocks and coffee cups. I spit soap bubbles. I turn into a train that goes along without knowing where to stop. I transform myself into a writing machine and it writes whatever I want it to write. I ravenously attack an ant, and start plucking out hairs from my armpit. A little hair removal. I pluck out footprints. Chills. Certainties. Things I should do. I pull out ferocious eels and cover my belly with candyfloss.

It's June.

They're having a *festa junina*[13] in the asylum.

The square-dancing lunatics are all in a line. The ones who take Gardenal don't speak. Others take Haldol. Others are drug addicts. Others could kill for a *cachaça* and play snooker. No one wants to join the line and dance. No psychotic wants to dance. No dimwit wants to stop banging his head against the wall. But Rimbaud is happy and dances without any sadness. There he is, if you pardon my bluntness, with the knife between his teeth. He's a gypsy spirit, the spirit of an Indian. Spirit of a pig. Thorn. Leprosy. AIDS. The silence of quicklime and myrtle, hollyhocks among the garden herbs. Rimbaud embroiders frangipani flowers on a straw cloth. Seven birds in the colours of the prism fly on the grey spider. Two horsemen gallop by Rimbaud's eyes: Baudelaire and me. Everything that kills passes by me. What is this? Cocaine or ether? What is this new sound? Drums. I can't dance, I can't dance. He's my friend, finally – a friend. *Acugêlê banzai!* I spit up into the air and open an umbrella. Baudelaire spits as he speaks. I use the umbrella to protect myself. Spits and sputters.

I was ordered to be here. I didn't want to come. I don't want to stay, for fuck's sake! Tell them I'm

Charles Laughton, for fuck's sake! Haven't they ever seen a film? The abandoned ones would have a better life outside. Even I would. Let's say I'm spending a season in hell, a season in my temples with my poet and actor friends. Tomorrow I'll forget about them, but they'll be back the day after tomorrow. I know they'll never abandon me. That's what friends are for, right? The street cleaner invites me to eat a box of Segredo biscuits with him. Life is a secret for me. I don't know exactly what it means. In the outside world I look for my name in the obituaries every day. I've already decided: I don't want to go to my funeral. I wonder what heaven for objects is like? Heaven for clocks, for TVs, computers, sling-shots, forks, knives, spoons. We only have spoons here. No one eats with a knife and fork. They eat with their mouths open, except Granny who eats a bit like my grandmother; she's skinny, soft, sweet. And one more very important detail: she gives me a kiss every time she passes by. I don't really care much for kisses. Rimbaud forced me to kiss him on the lips once. I've told him, it's no use, I can't be what I'm not.

Who knows, Rimbaud, maybe Verlaine will come along and fix that.

Baudelaire appears wearing boxing gloves. Baudelaire is nearly always an annoying, cranky prick. And strong. I almost, almost, never say yes to Baudelaire. Rimbaud's dirty. He needs to take a shower. Like Foucault always said, a good shower is a cold shower. Every lunatic should take a cold shower before bed. Electroshock comes from thermal shock.

The cold invites the fire. Jump over the bonfire, Rimbaud.

Jump, you bastard!

A dimwit and a bipolar woman are married by a hot psychologist. There are some good doctors. Most of the doctors are nice. My dad comes by. My sister comes by. My brother, my sister, Adélia and Anália, our sweet maids, with the strength of a thousand Haldols.

I'm sad and everyone is happy.

I'm reminded of the *festas juninas* of my childhood.

Because I'm fat, I dance with the fattest girl. That's life. Fatty with fatty. Skinny with skinny. Ugly with ugly. Pretty with pretty. I'd like the prettiest girl. I want to screw the psychologist. That's life. Lunatic with lunatic.

They made a huge bonfire out of paper and the lunatics' dirty nappies.

That guy who dared to leap over the flames got taken up the arse by the huge blaze of shit. That's what yesterday was like. And that's what today is like. Nothing changes. When you're a kid. When you're an adult. Life drains away into the sea through a sewer pipe. Thank goodness the sea is green, the colour of my brother Bruno's eyes. His eyes are clear, free of suffering. If you don't suffer, you're not alive. If you're alive, you eat French fries. It's a good thing there are always French fries to ease the burden. The days are all alike and keep repeating themselves. No one ever asks nicely if they can enter my life, but they always find an excuse to leave. Neon veins remind me of the signs I saw in New York with Rimbaud. Now that would make a good chapter title: the poets in New York. I can see myself lost in Columbia University or even in Harlem. Here we go: I'd be the king of Harlem. I'd screw the little Jewish chicks and kill the Irish bootleggers. Then I'd say: this is my motherfucking territory, bitch!

I take my pills with a Coke. The coconut sweets travel up my veins. The peanut brittle arrived dirty. Some idiot might think I'm lost in this party, dancing with the fattest girl in the room. I wanted to dance with Clarissa. I wanted to dance with the psychologist. But Granny lets loose, dancing down on the ground. Can she get back up? Only with a winch.

Call the paramedics, quickly, please. Actually, better call the cops.

•

Focus. Out of focus. I'm blind.

Deaf and dumb. My nerves are lit up but everything's dark.

Fearsome Madman appears in my dreams. He says Rosebud killed me. My head's exploding. Who killed Fearsome? The foetid veins in my head scan my speech. Rimbaud wants to marry me. Baudelaire is neurasthenic; he's always distant, even at the party. He's not going to found modernity with that perspective.

So I say to him: let's be modern, Baudelaire.

It was only then that he saw the girl passing by him. She was the *passante*. Later he told me that he never saw her again. God, Baudelaire is difficult! He likes to watch the girls go by in skimpy bikinis on the beach. It was only after Baudelaire that Vínicius de Moraes wrote 'The Girl from Ipanema'. The girl who when she passes, makes each one she passes go Ahh is the passer-by, for fuck's sake! The sea always beats down on the rocks of illness. The Lexotan 6 green sea. The Haldol 5 blue sky. The Rivotril white clouds. Everything is illness in mental illness, even the lovely Girl from Ipanema. Why haven't they come up with a cure for my illness?

Why are they building rockets to go into space?

I have a delusional episode while Alfonso appears

and tells me he's going to Paracambi. God, that guy should just go fuck off.

To keep repeating that ditty.

Poor thing.

I wouldn't wish being pitied, being seen as a poor bastard, on anyone. I'm not asking to have a place in heaven because I'm a poor bastard – far from it. I want to have the same look in my eyes that a lynx has for its prey. That Rimbaud has for his Abyssinia. Baudelaire's movement and his beautiful flowers. I can't stand taking the role of the victim. My role is the toilet roll. I'm a child and I don't know the truth. The truth, out there, is in the eyes of my brother Bruno, who doesn't know or care about anything. He lives happily with his nothingness. Everyone has nothingness.

I'm not nothing, Rimbaud. Want a cigarette?

I'll never be nothing. I can't want to be nothing.

Besides, I've got all the pills in the world inside me.

Rimbaud, I'll always be the one 'who wasn't born for this', I'll always be the one who waited for a door to open up for him in a wall without a door.

Rimbaud, we're bored of this party now, right? Baudelaire even wrote a poem. As for us, nothing. Although that story about New York might be interesting. What do you think?

•

The fat girl who danced with me explodes à la Mr Creosote.

Her body, her guts, displayed on my chest. Her chest on my chest. She keeps dancing. Just her legs. Granny keeps dancing and I try to keep up. I'm not good at this. I miss Mr Creosote's daughter. Miss Creosote.

I didn't want to dance with her, but I didn't want her to explode like that.

Her bits spread about all over the place.

I want a milkshake.

People who eat a lot don't know what they're eating. People who travel a lot don't know where they live. Every time I take a trip I mess up. I throw shit into the fan of sanity. One time I went down to Rio Grande do Sul. A friend of mine lived there. He played drums in my rock band. He was fat just like I am today. He had a love hotel there in Rio Grande do Sul. His hotel was quite different from the asylum. He went to all the brothels.

I'd already swallowed the cricket quite some time before that. I was twenty-one. It was my second sneak preview of hell.

On the first day, Rimbaud, we went to the local brothel. Back then whores didn't kiss.

Nowadays they do everything. They might even pay you to have sex with them.

Why are whores so clingy and so needy for love?
I don't like whores very much.

I like to give and feel pleasure.

I had a girlfriend at the time. She had blue eyes.
They were the most beautiful blue eyes in the world.
Even so, I went down to Rio Grande do Sul. When
I tried to kiss the whore she blocked my hand. You
can't mess with my stuff. You have to pay. Paying
for sex wasn't part of my plan. I'd planned on flying
the aeroplane of pleasure with her.

We left the brothel with four whores. *Acugêlê
banzai!*

A long, long time ago I went to Korea. It was really
different from Rio Grande do Sul. Every place I went
looked like an asylum. There was a nuclear bomb
there. One hell of a mess.

My friend wanted to have a drunken orgy. I
wasn't really into that. I was a bit of a prude. Maybe
today, after many orgies with Rimbaud and Baudelaire, I could have one with my friend. But I was
barely in my twenties, just a kid. I wanted to have
the whore all to myself. I wanted that whore with the
feather touch. We got in the car. How many rooms
does your house have? What does your mum do? I
had my eye on the hotel maid, too.

While the hands of the least pretty whore ran up and down me, in my friend's Ford Landau, I got paranoid, because her hands were rough. I started to think she was a transvestite. What had happened to the feather touch? Pure paranoia.

Paranoia. My psychiatrist at the time had given me Melleril.

But I didn't like the colour of the pill. A sort of peanut brown, a shit brown. Roberto Carlos[14] used to dress in brown, then he started wearing blue and his luck changed. What had he done to lose his OCD? I have my own. I don't like three, I prefer four.

When I told Rimbaud that story about Roberto Carlos and the one about my numbers, he recommended two books of poetry to me: *Trilce* and *Quaderna*.[15] One for three, another for four.

For God's sake, Rimbaud, don't put me in a bind. I'd rather use numbers for Kabbalah, not for poetry.

Unfortunately he only taught me what he knew, and he didn't know much. That was when he told me about maybe going back to Africa, for his leg to get better.

Let's get back to the hotel.

My friend told me that I had to vacate one of the rooms and stay where the staff sleep.

Tonight you're going to sleep here in the same room as Stallion. He's going to hang you up by your little tits. Stallion was a big black man standing over six and a half feet tall. Rumour had it that Stallion had a dick so big he could have been a porn star. I just dabbled in sex with my little 15-cm-edition, PG-rated knob. I trembled the first time I saw Stallion. I wasn't going to sleep next to that guy. He could easily rape me. When I saw Stallion again, I thought about getting out of there. I told myself: I'm not waiting for the third time, or else I won't see anything ever again, just the spirit of the god of evil moving upon the face of the waters of Lake Guaíba.

I left the hotel and went to the bus station. I was possessed by a fertile spirit of modern madness, one that had helped twentieth-century poetry many times and had put contemporary literature in its rightful place. My persecution complex had reached the pinnacle of its glory. I ran through the streets of Porto Alegre. The police saw me running. Police are automatons. They're like scarecrows. Scarecrows with no eyes. And ravens peck at scarecrows. I was a solitary raven that night. Cops are the same all over the world. They shot at me. Mint bullets, peanut bullets, soft bullets. And rubber bullets.

Stop, for fuck's sake!

I stopped. There was a police station close to the bus station.

Own up, you piece of shit. You got drugs on you?

What's the problem? None. I was embarrassed to tell the police about the god of evil. I was embarrassed to tell them the truth about the fertile spirit of modern madness, the one that had already written a very important chapter in that century's literature. I still had a drop of discretion at that point.

You're not from around here. I'm from Rio, but I'm a big fan of Getúlio Vargas' southern accent.

Are you a poet? For fuck's sake! Out with it! Or are you too delicate to talk?

Sir, I was going to be raped at the love hotel.

The police called the hotel. They quickly saw that it was unfounded. A delicate flower, said one. Anyway, they told me to go back there.

I couldn't do it. I spent the night at the police station and went back home the next day by plane.

My first and only plane trip. The trips to China, Japan and Korea were all by television. Now I'm here to stay, I told myself.

Rimbaud appeared out of the crowd. There was a crowd behind me. I hugged Rimbaud for the first time. I hugged the world and kept quiet.

Yes.

No.

I walked on and on. Wandering. Singing. Rimbaud by my side. He missed Verlaine. I missed Marina. People often miss when the match gets tight. He tripped me up. Rimbaud really was a bastard. I couldn't deny that he was one of my own.

The party was still going strong.

I ate black coconut sweets. Black things are so pretty, except for Stallion. There weren't any black pills. Black is just a lot of things. The black morning that devours me as I write my obituary. It's better to leave everything ready. Someone might forget I died. On a rainy day, I died like Vallejo. As a matter of fact, Rimbaud really insisted that I read *Trilce*. On a sunny day, a Thursday I think, I woke up in a bad mood. Every goal is a medal on your breast. The general has lots of medals and no wars. In São Paulo one time, a really powerful woman told me I'd been a soldier in another life. Many wars to be won. A kid who loved the Beatles and the Rolling Stones like me. Vietnam. It was in his blood. Helicopters all around. Napalm. Mustard gas. Bayonets stuck into bodies. Injecting some ferocious chemical.

Onward, the Maltese Falcon says to Charles.

Attack on the left flank. It was my chance to turn into Humphrey Bogart. Troops ready. *Acugêlê banzai!*

Crazy Nerd and Silver Alky were playing *Battleship*. What do I know about war? Guerrilla tactics. Silence. Who's afraid? Surging adrenaline and the smell of manure attack me as I blink. Strobe light. Black light. Spots. Thunderclaps. Lightning and rain. It's raining now. It always rains when I want it to. Rain? There's no rain falling . . . So how do I feel one day when the sound of rain attracts my useless agony? Where does it rain, where is it sad? Tell me, clear sky. I make it rain. I'm strong enough. But I'm fragile and delicate like anyone who feels life. Not everybody knows what they want out of life. If you do know, you live life. If you don't, you feel life.

I miss Rimbaud. I guess I'm going to lose a friend. He's not been around. Baudelaire never was much for having a chat. I think he really does think I'm Charles Laughton, Hunchback of Notre-Dame.

I never knew when he was close by.

The stars are up there, Baudelaire.

They've gone now.

I hope that when the Big Bang happens, a spaceship full of earthlings will be shot into outer space, taking at least one Van Gogh painting with it.

He chewed on his ear until the end of his days. He'd been through hell. He was born to be wild and a hero.

From white to black. Let's be realistic.

The things we invent are all Carnival costumes. Some costumes might be better than others. Sometimes they might even be tragic. Being tragic is worse than being crazy. Only Fearsome Madman is both tragic and crazy. Could I have been the one who killed Fearsome?

I want to be promoted to someone's hallucination, please!

To fly in a helicopter. I'm going to be a pilot, Dad. Being delicate cost me my life.

[FROM GREEK *EPILOGOS*]

Everything goes out. The candles go out. The matches go out. I don't even know if it's sunny outside. I smoke a cigarette that doesn't go out. I drink a smoothie from back when they didn't make me fat. She tells me I'm cute. I leave myself behind two hundred times a day and I come back. Each time I go out a little bit less. Countdown. Five, four, three, two, one. I went from infinity to infamy. From infamy to infinity. There was the smell of Mum's orange cake in the air. Friday.

When I got home I'd never heard so much silence in my room. I'd been released just a few hours earlier. This time no one had tailed our car. I hadn't seen Rimbaud or Baudelaire for a few days. When you have such strong ties and you shared a life together, you miss your friends. My blue dog was there, grubby with age, with lots of stories to tell.

I walked around my house and felt free. Freedom was in the small things: reading emails, opening the fridge. Now I needed to get healthier. Open things. I opened the box of matches. I opened the gas valve and lit the flame. I opened the box of incense. I went along opening, opening, opening, as if I were opening up and discovering things for the first time. It felt like I'd spent a century away from home. Everything was the same, but different.

I was a butterfly butterflying around the minefield, the power zone, the place where all my scandals had played out. I was back to my life.

I put a pizza in the oven. Finally I could eat something that appealed to me. I devoured the pizza like a Viking eating roast quail. Then I lay down to sleep.

The meds made me shiver and drool.

Night came quickly. I put away a plate of veg and salad, for a snack. I went to my room and slept.

Men with manes, bird manes, were speaking a language I didn't understand. I had a strange theory: every animal on earth has a planet where its intelligence is equal to that of humans and they survive like us. So, beetles had Beetleland; ducks, Duckland. Maybe I was just dreaming about Disneyland? There was a league that brought together all the beings in the universe. But each one spoke its own language. *K d pocua besourfez biologic Todog.*

I woke up suddenly, the word *Todog* echoing in my ears. I wrote down the code and stuck it on the corkboard. The dream would recur, but always with a new word. I felt special, receiving those messages. I thought I was a clairvoyant, all-seeing. Someone who'd have answers for the cosmos. I placed an ad in the newspaper, looking for other people who had the same powers, who were working in the same field.

Ten people appeared. We decided to hold meetings called Todog. We were tasked with creating a new language that different beings would use to communicate with one another.

The meetings were delightful, each of us talking about our life with extraterrestrials. Some had had chips implanted, so we needed to join together as a congregation. We ate wind. We drank air. We fed on sunlight. I lost thirty kilos. We started to set aside some money for our photocopying expenses and supplies.

Out of the Todog meetings came the Todog religion. I was consecrated Magma I. And each one of the other ten members had a specific role. It was a small step from my consecration as Magma I to being First Todog.

Rising over other people is a funny thing. Having the power to speak and make others do exactly what you've asked. But I didn't abuse my status as First Todog.

I was the First Todog, the one everyone had to respect. I was a kind of god to those people. I was responsible for making sense of the laws of the universe and turning them into a language that could be understood by the other beings in the universe.

For my father this was pure insanity.

You want me to call you Todog. Like a kind of dog?

No, not dog. It's Todog.

How ridiculous can you be. Look at you, wearing a robe. You don't even put on trousers any more.

They're Todog robes.

And the flowers?

Todog flowers.

Everything is Todog?

Yes, I'm part of everything. *Anhamambé arlicouse proto bumba Todog.*

Stop saying that nonsense.

To cantilya chamtipa cur
Tuereriçaau mandique puss
Pos polacossidrometáuio.

Todog.

My father slapped me across the face. The other members of my religion laid into my father.

They really beat me up. I'm calling the police.

We have religious freedom.

Your religion is lynching an old man.

When they attack our god Todog we're defending ourselves from their hell.

My hell is all of you and this idiot son of mine.

Todog. We are one another's hell.

I'm kicking you out. Go live in some other shithole.

Todog. Absentam. Clux.

Todog.

I left and went to the streets preaching the Todog. First we had to grow and multiply the number of the faithful.

We got into a fight on the corner of Miguel Lemos with some punks who were passing by. Todog is strong and imposes itself by force. Two punks converted. The power of the word renewed the lives of those who took on the teachings.

We went to sleep in a nearby shelter. I had to name a Todog 2 to take my place. So I chose the fattest one. I called him Xuma Quizombe. Xuma consecrated himself grand master. *Bencotuzaac maarrienovic gossstumaan.* Xuma Todog 2. He was my secretary on all our works. Kicked out of the shelter, we went to an abandoned campground.

In two months there were 500 of us.

Todog Xantipa maarlameeu.

With time, I was feeling my body less and less. They gave me some other glasses and these new glasses gave me strange powers. Like concentrating solely and exclusively on my destiny. After all, it's not like everyone has gone through what I have. And I needed to forget everything, remember less, not live in the past so much. Dogs were blue and what would this lead to? It wasn't my fault that I saw the light of things. Although the light of things was disappearing and giving way to a new light: the *Todog lutz vaticerum forbid beach boys club.*

With time, I was starting to master the language. The one that would unite all beings. I knew the language so well that I was slowly giving up speaking my own language. The meetings at the campground were fruitful. I spoke to more and more people.

You need to deliver your self to Todog. The world was made for you. A calm world of love. *Fortex climberg Todog.*

There were times when I only spoke Todog and Xuma translated for everyone. The people made donations. So many that we bought the campground and built a big house there.

Go to bed. This is no hour for a child to be up.

Yes, Mum.

I slept with my blue dog.

You have a very beautiful future ahead of you, the fortune teller told me.

She read the lines on the palm of my hand.

Our house was new. A dog always came along and howled in the mirrored night that was the lake. Every lake is a mirrored night when the moon is full.

The furious hands of silence were falling through my childhood. The deeper I got into my childhood Todog, the more I forgot myself. Gradually I forgot that I had a family. My family became Todog. During the sermons I emphasised the need to love your neighbour as yourself. I wrote a booklet with some commandments. And I also set down rules for our use of psychotropic drugs. After a month we had over a thousand followers. We lived off what we grew in the big vegetable garden on the old campground. We built houses. Many rich people joined the ranks of Todog and donated lots of money to help make it an official foundation. Over time it became necessary to put some controls in place. Each new member had to spend one month weeding, the next one planting, and so on and so forth. Since Todog was only revealed to me, I was the one who doled out punishments.

One fine day some cops came and took me to a nearby asylum. In the asylum I was put in the ward for the most serious cases.

A crowd was shouting outside the asylum. More than a thousand. Xuma is commanding the picket line. Slowly the police start to arrive. They want order. Todog isn't about violence. The police start to let fly. Knocking people senseless left, right and centre. The Todog retaliate. The police fire tear gas at my people.

Inside the asylum the lunatics are frightened. They put me in a skip and transfer me to a prison.

You're leading a band of lunatics.

They're not lunatics.

They're following a lunatic like you.

Surely we're not causing any harm.

Xuma shows up, bloodied, and gives me a hug.

Todog.

What the hell is that? What's Todog?

Todog is all the forces in one.

Spit it out.

Todog is the language that all animals speak.

You trying to say that dogs don't bark?

Dogs and all living beings have a transcendent home of their own.

The officer called another cop and had him bring in the most ferocious dog in the regiment. The dog entered, barking and slobbering, a ball of rage beside me.

Todog ministral calipsomburguer veneran do lupsier todog.

The dog, who was about to bite me, started licking me, docility itself. I turned to the cops:

This is Todog. The language all understand.

Our man here is crazy. He's screwing with us. The dog doesn't understand that shit, no way.

The cop pistol-whipped me and my eyebrow started to bleed. Xuma ran towards me. They clobbered him with the pistol too.

We're going to keep you here under arrest for now.

And Xuma?

The pair of you will be here for a while now.

The officer took us to a storeroom and started laying into us. Beat us until we bled. Until our noses were bloody. I kept telling Xuma that Todog didn't allow violence and we couldn't react if we were truly men of faith. I asked why they were doing it and they said they didn't know why they were beating us, but we knew why we were being beaten.

Todog stuff.

It was a way to ease our guilt and our pain.

We were taken before the judge and sentenced to four years for sedition. The first thing I thought of was Todog. In those four years what would become of the hundreds of people who had believed in me?

All dogs are blue? I swallowed a chip. I swallowed a cricket. What else is left to devour in this world?

Carnival only wears the colours of short-lived happiness. Dealing with lunatics or with normal people: what's the difference? What is reality? How many pieces of wood do you need to make that canoe? How many mortars do you need to sink that boat?

At times like these I get to thinking about my mum and the orange cake she would make every Friday. Rimbaud and Baudelaire never visited me again. Either I'm cured or even crazier. I'm more locked away than ever. No one ever does the right thing, however much they try. How is it my fault that I'm locked up? Rimbaud: why don't you come around to cheer me up? I've been abandoned. Baudelaire: you're a bore, but you write well. Drop by, both of you. Come over. You guys cut me off without warning. Some rats scuttle between my cell and Xuma's cell. *Todog apartenum politicum est.* The rats form a circle and dance the can-can.

I saw an Umbanda[16] ritual that day. A decapitated chicken. A goat was sacrificed and I was soaked in blood. I was fifteen and I swallowed a cricket, then I saved the house from the termites. Four years in here.

Fourth of November: the day I was born. No cake and no party. Nothing.

I got a tricycle, but the neighbour already had a bicycle. I want a bicycle, a bicycle without training wheels, so I can learn how to fall. Happiness.

Hi, you've just received an important email: take Viagra.

Every being – no matter how nasty – had a childhood, had an adolescence. How do these facts affect adult life? Could my childhood have determined who I'd turn out to be? I was a quiet boy. Had a faraway look. Sometimes I wonder, given how many problems I've got, whether my parents didn't hide something from me. I didn't fool around with guys. I wasn't molested. I dated a pretty girl. I had everything I wanted. Why had fate done this to me? What was Hitler's childhood like?

Xuma looks at me and says something in Todog. For four years we only spoke in Todog.

Four years passed quickly. We were put in with the most dangerous prisoners. But thankfully the days flew by. In the meantime, the Todogs on the outside multiplied. To the point where, thanks to the right of freedom to worship, Todog was accepted as a religion. Three days before I got out, people were already gathering at rallies to hear the few words I'd taught.

We're heroes, said Xuma.

We are.

Our people out there are organised; who do you think took our places?

No one, Xuma.

When we stepped out into freedom, a radio station immediately asked what message I'd like to give at that moment:

Todog olambolic Todog.

What does it mean?

We don't usually translate. Either the words enter you or they don't. Xuma understands me, don't you Xuma?

Yes, Todog.

Some familiar faces, armed with banners and posters, were outside waiting for us. The familiar faces greeted us, revered us, idolised us and showed themselves to be faithful to Todog. I was impressed when they said there were ten thousand people waiting in Getúlio, wanting to hear my prayers.

Some familiar faces gave us white, tight-fitting clothes, just like everyone now wore.

We reached the gates of the farm in Getúlio and there were a lot of people jostling around. Some familiar faces inside the car showed me that the tax payments were up to date and the farm was legal.

Xamarei kodof pluicinai orlandopen rictimu asimbandueira pepinovic astrolov erguirochonte. Ritmos lacrimai rictyuliberius profteriobarto labaredasava perbuliam Todog.

Todog.

Todog morten Todog livus.

Todog.

•

Some even more familiar faces took us back. We drove through the crowd with the top down. They threw things at me. Underwear, bras, letters, posters, pieces of paper, confetti, streamers, guitars, bottles, plastic cups. I stood up and waved to the crowd. All of a sudden, a crazy Todog fundamentalist got up close to the car and shot me twice. They grabbed the man and he screamed, saying he was Todog.

I struggled between life and death. I fought with the help of the doctors and drugs, but I didn't make it. At my funeral, Xuma said that Todog died with me. Even so, many people still say they follow Todog.

Princilimpimpotus todog todog todog and crickets and electrodes and a house in ruins and a blue dog and an orange cake and B Cops and Granny and I'm going to Paracambi if I don't eat, I'll go to Caju and Attorney General Brylcreem and Xuma and now the now. D-Day. The moment of truth. The bomb and its mushroom cloud of endorphins explode in my bayoneted body with the chemical of the angels. The warhead. And then, Rodrigo? What did you do with the after? Here where the clouds meet I always get a bigger shock than the ones I got in the asylum.

Where I am now all the dogs aren't blue. They gave me a third pair of glasses, third eye. Third ear. A third arm. Third leg. A third hand. All in threes. Then they gave me two more penises. Two more noses. Another foot. Two more stomachs. My third life.

Three Hail Marys.

I had to get used to my new life and what's worse is I still haven't turned into a monster because of it.

I'm still the boy with the blue dog. A great big blue reflected now in the eyes of the boy who found my blue dog in the rubbish.

PUBLISHER'S PREFACE TO
THE SECOND BRAZILIAN EDITION
OF *ALL DOGS ARE BLUE*

This book has a long, difficult history.

I received the manuscript of the first version of *All Dogs are Blue* in 2003, and was blown away when I read it. We weren't able to invest in its publication at the time (the usual challenges of distributing and marketing first-time authors), but I got in touch with Rodrigo to let him know how much I'd liked the text; to discuss a partnership that would let us explore alternative publishing options; and to encourage him to send it along to other, bigger publishers, as it was one of the best manuscripts I'd ever laid hands on.

During that first conversation, I made a commitment to publish the book as soon we could afford it – something that would only come about five years later, thanks in part to a grant from Petrobras which enabled Rodrigo to work on the final version of his text, and us at 7Letras, his publisher, to produce an initial print run of 1,500 copies.

Over the years, we talked a few times on the phone (he never left the house) and I was struck by how lucidly and clearly he spoke about his condition – the schizophrenia, the medication, his paranoia, the hospitalisations – which only increased my admiration for his talent and his art.

During the time we worked on the book, Rodrigo's closest contact at 7Letras was with Valeska de Aguirre, who edited the text and became a sort of friend. The two spoke almost daily, always by phone, as well as exchanging extensive emails about Rodrigo's other literary projects, which were to remain posthumous.

Only on the day we launched *All Dogs are Blue*, at a signing in the playground of the building where Rodrigo lived with his family, did he and I finally meet in person. On that day it became clear that his work – which he had already begun to share on the internet – was getting recognition from several people in the literary world. Rodrigo himself purchased a sizeable share of books from that first imprint to send to various critics, writers and journalists, always trusting his own instincts.

A few months later came the announcement that the book had been nominated as one of fifty finalists for the Portugal Telecom Prize. On the night that the longlist was announced, his book was specifically cited (alongside the names of some of the most prominent names in Portuguese-language literature) as a sign of renewal and originality in Brazilian literature. The next day I rang Rodrigo – who by then was getting out of the house more, taking a painting course at an art school – to tell him the good news. During the course of the phone call he became very emotional, his voice cracked, and all he could say was 'so much suffering'. He repeated the phrase and then couldn't carry on, and I may also have choked up before we rang off.

News of Rodrigo's death fell like a bombshell on 7Letras. It confirmed, somehow, the author's own prediction (in a message that mixed his delirious lucidity with a dash of irony) that his books would only become successful after his death. In life, I think he was at least able to take in the positive reactions of those first readers and critics, who realised the strength and scope of his potent prose.

I wasn't able to share with Rodrigo the joy of seeing the book's first edition sell out (a rare success for a newcomer in Brazil, still a country of few readers), but I can imagine he would feel happy and fulfilled to see this new edition in circulation, coming to life with each new reader – just as I imagine each new reader will feel the same impact that I felt upon discovering this incredibly dense, rich and original work, which I continue to appreciate more fully with each new reading.

Jorge Viveiros de Castro, 2010
Publisher, 7Letras

NOTES

1 *It's only Tupi in Anhembi*. The Tupi indigenous peoples occupied much of the territory that is now Brazil when the Portuguese arrived in 1500. European diseases and slavery largely wiped out the indigenous population, but the mixed-race descendants of Portuguese settlers and indigenous women – known as *mamelucos* – kept the Tupi heritage alive and well. Indeed, until the Marquis of Pombal made Portuguese teaching mandatory in Brazilian schools in 1750, the Tupi language formed the basis for the country's earlier lingua franca, Nheengatu, and its close southern relative, the Língua Geral Paulista.

Anhembi is a small town in the state of São Paulo. It so happens that its patron is Our Lady of Remedies. The word 'Anhembi' is of Tupi derivation.

The narrator is also alluding to Oswald de Andrade's 1928 'Cannibal Manifesto', one of the most important texts of Brazilian modernism, which includes the English phrase: 'Tupi or not Tupi, that is the question.' The manifesto argues that cannibalism has been misrepresented by sensationalist accounts: cannibals may ritually eat an enemy or an important ancestor, but in both cases it will be someone they revere. By eating the respected person the cannibals take the person's strength into themselves. Andrade suggests the strength of Brazilian culture lies in its ability to 'digest' foreign influences without being dominated by them.

2   *Paracambi.* A town in the state of Rio de Janeiro and home to a number of psychiatric clinics. The town's name is also of Tupi derivation, and means, roughly, 'the green forest by the sea'.

3   *the elastic, bovine drool that writer talks about.* 'That writer' is the Brazilian journalist, playwright and author Nelson Rodrigues (1912–1980).

4   *Casas da Banha.* A Brazilian supermarket chain in the 1980s and 1990s; the name means, literally, Houses of Lard. The chain was based in Rio, where many people still remember it. It was one of the first to have hypermarkets in Brazil, including their flagship store Porcão (literally: the big pig).

5   *Caju.* A reference to São Francisco Xavier Cemetery, more commonly known in Rio as Caju Cemetery.

6   *I'm leaving for Pasargadae.* The English translation of 'Vou-me embora pra Pasárgada' – a well-known poem by Brazilian writer Manuel Bandeira (1886–1968). In it, the poet imagines escaping to the ancient Persian city of Pasargadae, which he reimagines as a utopian land: 'Lá sou amigo do rei / Lá tenho a mulher que eu quero / Na cama que escolherei' (There, I am the king's friend / Have the woman I want / In the bed that I choose). Translation by ABM Cadaxa (*Oasis* 1973).

7   *Iansan.* (Iansã in Portuguese.) A spirit entity, or Orisha, of the Afro-Brazilian religious faith Candomblé. She is invoked

with the phrase *Epahei, Iansan!*, which is not Portuguese, but comes from the Yoruba.

8   *I watched Esper on TV.* Ronaldo Esper is a well-known Brazilian fashion and bridal designer who has appeared regularly on TV programmes since the late 1990s, and is famous for his scathing verdicts on Brazilian celebrities' fashion sense.

9   *'Boemia'.* A song by Teodoro and Sampaio, an extremely popular duo who sing *sertanejo* music – a genre of kitsch, romantic, acoustic guitar music that is rich in double entendres. The *sertanejo* is, literally, a person from the *sertão*, the outback in the North-east of Brazil.

10   *National Kid and the Venusian Incas. National Kid* (or *Nacional Kid,* as it was known in Brazil) was a Japanese TV series produced by Toei Company in 1960 and commissioned by Panasonic, then called National. The series never took off in Japan or the rest of the world, but was big in Brazil. Over the course of many series, our hero faced and defeated several enemies. The first of these were the Venusian Incas, who appeared in a flying saucer from outer space and threatened Japan with malevolent deeds.

11   *Acugêlê banzai.* A reference to the poem 'Não sei dançar' (I Can't Dance) by Manuel Bandeira, in which he describes a cross-section of Brazilian society dancing to a jazz band at a Carnival party. One of the dancers is a Japanese man: 'O japonês também dança maxixe / Acugêlê banzai!' (The Japanese man dances maxixe too / Acugêlê banzai!). The poet has brought together 'Acugêlê', an African interjection not commonly used in Brazil, and 'banzai', a Japanese war cry. 'Maxixe' is a Brazilian dance

115

that developed towards the end of the nineteenth century and was also known as the Brazilian tango.

12   *One takes ether. The other, cocaine.* A second allusion to Manuel Bandeira's 'Não sei dançar'. It starts: 'Uns tomam éter, outros cocaína / Eu já tomei tristeza, hoje tomo alegria' (Some take ether, others cocaine / I've already taken sadness, today I'm taking joy).

13   *festa junina.* National celebrations of popular saints that take place every June, coinciding with the winter solstice.

14   *Roberto Carlos.* Often called 'The King', Roberto Carlos is a famous Brazilian pop singer whose career has spanned over fifty years.

15   *Trilce and Quaderna. Trilce,* by the Peruvian poet César Vallejo (1892–1938), is a seminal work of modernist, avant-garde poetry. In one version of events, Vallejo decided to name the work *Trilce* after listening to his printer repeatedly mis-pronounce the Spanish word *tres,* meaning three. *Quaderna,* by one of the greatest Latin American poets, the Brazilian João Cabral de Melo Neto (1920–1999), is written entirely in four-line stanzas.

16   *Umbanda.* A Brazilian religion believed to have originated in Rio de Janeiro that blends elements of African religions, Catholicism, spiritism and various indigenous beliefs. It bears some similarities to other Afro-Brazilian religions such as Candomblé.

TRANSLATORS'
ACKNOWLEDGEMENTS

A special thank you to my husband and navigator,
Bruno, for his advice, support and infectious enthusiasm.

Zoë Perry

Many thanks to Ana Amália Alves, whose invaluable
knowledge and advice helped me negotiate the subtleties
of Rodrigo de Souza Leão's style and humour.

Stefan Tobler

Dear readers,

We rely on subscriptions from people like you to tell these other stories – the types of stories most UK publishers would consider too risky to take on.

Our subscribers don't just make the books physically happen. They also help us approach booksellers, because we can demonstrate that our books already have readers and fans. And they give us the security to publish in line with our values, which are collaborative, imaginative and 'shamelessly literary' (the *Guardian*).

All of our subscribers:

- receive a first edition copy of every new book we publish
- are thanked by name in the books
- are warmly invited to contribute to our plans and choice of future books

BECOME A SUBSCRIBER, OR GIVE A SUBSCRIPTION TO A FRIEND

Visit andotherstories.org/subscribe to become part of an alternative approach to publishing.

Subscriptions are:

£20 for two books per year

£35 for four books per year

£50 for six books per year

The subscription includes postage to Europe, the US and Canada. If you're based anywhere else, we'll charge for postage separately.

OTHER WAYS TO GET INVOLVED

If you'd like to know about upcoming events and reading groups (our foreign-language reading groups help us choose books to publish, for example) you can:

- join the mailing list at: andotherstories.org/join-us
- follow us on twitter: @andothertweets
- join us on Facebook: And Other Stories

This book was made possible thanks to the support of:

AS Byatt
Abigail Headon
Adam Biles
Adam Lenson
Adam Mars-Jones
Adrian Ford
Adrian May
Ailsa Holland
Ajay Sharma
Alan Bowden
Alannah Hopkin
Alasdair Thomson
Alastair Dickson
Alastair Gillespie
Alastair Kenny
Alastair Laing
Aldo Peternell
Alec Begley
Alex Gregory
Alex H Wolf
Alex Read
Alex Webber &
    Andy Weir
Alexander Bryan
Alexandra de
    Verseg-Roesch
Ali Conway
Ali Smith
Ali Usman
Alice Nightingale
Alison Anderson
Alison Bennets
Alison Hughes
Alison Layland
Alison Macdonald

Alison Scanlon
Alison Winston
Alistair Shaw
Allison Graham
Amanda Banham
Amy Capelin
Amy Crofts
Ana Amália Alves
Andrea Davis
Andrew Robertson
Andrew Clarke
Andrew Marston
Andrew Nairn
Andrew Wilkinson
Angela Jane Fountas
Angela Jane
    Mackworth-Young
Angela Thirlwell
Angus MacDonald
Anna Britten
Anna Milsom
Anna Vinegrad
Anna-Karin Palm
Annabel Hagg
Annalise Pippard
Anne & Ian
    Davenport
Anne Carus
Anne Claire Le Reste
Anne Longmuir
Anne Marie Jackson
Anne Meadows
Anne Okotie
Anne Withers
Anne Woodman

Annette Morris
    & Jeff Dean
Annette Nugent
Annie Henriques
Annie Ward
Anoushka Athique
Anthony Messenger
Anthony Quinn
Aquila Ismail
Archie Davies
Asher Norris
Averill Buchanan

Barbara Latham
Barbara Mellor
Barbara Adair
Barbara Zybutz
Bartolomiej Tyszka
Ben Thornton
Ben Coles
Ben Smith
Ben Ticehurst
Benjamin Judge
Benjamin Morris
Bettina Debon
Blanka Stoltz
Brenda Scott
Brendan Franich
Brendan McIntyre
Bruce & Maggie
    Holmes
Bruce Ackers
Bruce Millar
Bruce Rodgers

CT Rowse
Camilla Cassidy
Cara & Bali Haque
Cara Eden
Carla Palmese
Carole JS Russo
Caroline Gregory
Caroline Perry
Caroline Rigby
Caroline Thompson
Carrie LaGree
Catherine Mansfield
Catherine Nightingale
Catherine Whelton
Cecile Baudry
Celine McKillion
Charles Beckett
Charles Day
Charles Lambert
Charles Rowley
Charlotte Holtam
Charlotte Middleton
Charlotte Ryland
Charlotte Whittle
Charlotte Williams
Chenxin Jiang
Chris Hemsley
Chris Day
Chris Gribble
Chris Stevenson
Chris Watson
Christina Baum
Christina
    MacSweeney
Christina Scholtz
Christine Luker

Christopher Allen
Christopher Butler
Christopher Marlow
Christopher Spray
Ciara Greene
Ciara Ní Riain
Claire Brooksby
Claire Tranah
Claire Williams
Clare Buckeridge
Clare Bowerman &
    Dan Becker
Clare Fisher
Clare Keates
Clarice Borges-Smith
Clifford Posner
Clive Bellingham
Clive Chapman
Colin Burrow
Collette Eales
Craig Barney

Daisy Aitchison
Daisy Meyland-Smith
Damien Tuffnell
Dan Powell
Daniel Carpenter
Daniel Hugill
Daniel James Fraser
Daniel JF Quinn
Daniel Ng
Daniel O'Donovan
Daniel Sheldrake
Daniela Steierberg
Dave Lander
David Dougan

David Hedges
David Herling
David Kelly
David & Ann Dean
David Archer
David Breuer
David Craig Hall
David Davenport
David Gould
David Hanson
David Hebblethwaite
David Humphries
David Johnson-Davies
David Roberts
Davida Murdoch
Debbie Pinfold
Deborah Smith
Diana Brighouse
Duarte Nunes

EJ Baker
E Jarnes
Eamonn Furey
Ebru & Jon
Eddie Dick
Eileen Buttle
Elaine Rassaby
Elaine Martel
Eleanor Maier
Elizabeth Boyce &
    Simon Ellis
Elizabeth Draper
Elizabeth Polonsky
Ellie Michell
Els van der Vlist &
    Elise Rietveld

Emily Jones
Emily Evans
Emily Jeremiah
Emily Rhodes
Emma Kenneally
Emma Teale
Eric Langley
Erin Barnes
Evgenia Loginova

Fawzia Kane
Federay Holmes
Fiona & Andrew
    Sutton
Fiona Quinn
Florian Andrews
Frances Chapman
Francesca Bray
Francis Taylor
Francisco Vilhena
Freddy Hamilton

Gabriela Saldanha
Gabrielle Crockatt
Gabrielle Morris
Gale Pryor
Galia Loya
Garry Wilson
Gavin Collins
Gavin Madeley
Gawain Espley
Gay O'Mahoney
Geoff Egerton
Geoff Thrower
Geoff Wood
George McCaig

George Sandison &
    Daniela Laterza
George Savona
George Wilkinson
Georgia Panteli
Georgina Forwood
Gerald Peacocke
Geraldine Brodie
Gesine Treptow
Gillian Doherty
Gillian Jondorf
Gillian Spencer
Gillian Stern
Giselle Maynard
Gloria Sully
Glynis Ellis
Gordon Cameron
Gordon Campbell
Gordon Mackechnie
Grace Cantillon
Graham & Steph
    Parslow
Graham Hardwick
Graham Lockie
Graham R Foster
Guy Haslam

Hannah & Matt Perry
Hannah Falvey
Hannah Perret
Hannes Heise
Harriet Mossop
Harriet Sayer
Helen Buck
Helen Collins
Helen Manders

Helen McMurray
Helen Morales
Helen Riglia
Helen Weir
Helen Wormald
Helena Taylor
Helene Walters
Hélène Steculorum-
    Decoopman
Henrike Laehnemann
Hercules Fisherman
Hilary McPhee
Howard Watson
Howdy Reisdorf
Hugh Buckingham

Ian Barnett
Ian Buchan
Ian Burgess
Ian McAlister
Ian McMillan
Ian Mulder
Imogen Forster
Inna Carson
Irene Mansfield
Isabel Costello
Isabella Garment
Isabelle Kaufeler
Isfahan Henderson
Isobel Dixon
Isobel Staniland

J Collins
J Ellis
JC Sutcliffe
Jack Brown

Jackie Andrade
Jacqueline Crooks
Jacqueline Lademann
Jacqueline Taylor
Jacquie Bloese
James Portlock
James Barlow
James Clark
James Cubbon
James Mutch
James Upton
Jane Brandon
Jane Heslop
Jane Packman
Jane Tappuny
Jane Whiteley
Jane Woollard
Janet Mullarney
Janette Ryan
Jeffrey & Emily Alford
Jen Hamilton-Emery
Jenifer Logie
Jennifer Campbell
Jennifer Hurstfield
Jenny McPhee
Jenny Diski
Jenny Dover
Jenny Kosniowski
Jenny Newton
Jerry Lynch
Jess Wood
Jill Aizlewood
Jillian Jones
Jim Boucherat
Jo Elvery
Jo Harding

Joanne Hart
Jocelyn English
Joel Love
Joel Norbury
Johan Forsell
Johannes Georg Zipp
John Allison
John Gent
John Glahome
John Nicholson
John Oven
John Conway
John Corrigan
John Kelly
Jon Lindsay Miles
Jonathan & Julie Field
Jonathan Evans
Jonathan Watkiss
Jorge Lopez
    de Luzuriaga
Joseph Cooney
JP Sanders
Judit & Nigel
Judy Jones
Judy Kendall
JUJU Sophie
Julia Sutton
Julia Carveth
Julia Humphreys
Julia Sandford-Cooke
Julian Duplain
Julian I Phillippi
Julian Lomas
Julie Begon
Julie Freeborn
Julie Gibson

Julie Van Pelt
Juliet Hillier
Juliet Swann
Justine Taylor

KL Ee
Kaite O'Reilly
Kaitlin Olson
Karan Deep Singh
Kasia Boddy
Kate Gardner
Kate Griffin
Kate Leigh
Kate Thompson
Katharine Robbins
Katherine El-Salahi
Katherine Jacomb
Kathryn Lewis
Kathy Owles
Katia Leloutre
Katie Martin
Katie Smith
Katrina Ritters
Keith Alldritt
Keith Dunnett
Keith Underwood
Kevin Acott
Kevin Brockmeier
Kevin Murphy
Kevin Pino
Kim Sanderson
Kristin Djuve
Kristina Fitzsimmons
Krystalli Glyniadakis

Lander Hawes

Laraine Poole
Larry Colbeck
Laura Bennett
Laura Jenkins
Laura Murdoch
Laura Solon
Laura Woods
Lauren Kassell
Lauren Hickey
Lauren Roberts-Sklar
Lea Beresford
Leanne Bass
Leni Shilton
Lesley Lawn
Lindsay Brammer
Lindsey Ford
Liz Clifford
Liz Ketch
Liz Tunnicliffe
Lizzi Wagner
Loretta Platts
Loretta Brown
Lorna Bleach
Lorna Scott Fox
Lorraine Curr
Louise Bongiovanni
Louise Rogers
Lucinda Smith
Lucy North
Lyn Abbotts
Lynda Graham
Lyndsey Cockwell
Lynn Martin

M Manfre
Madeleine Kleinwort

Maggie Peel
Maisie & Nick Carter
Malcolm Bourne
Malcolm Cotton
Mandy Boles
Mansur Quraishi
Marella Oppenheim
Marese Cooney
Margaret Jull Costa
Maria Elisa Moorwood
Maria Pelletta
Maria Potter
Marie Schallamach
Marie Therese Cooney
Marieke Vollering
Marina Castledine
Marion Cole
Marion Tricoire
Mark Ainsbury
Mark Blacklock
Mark Howdle
Mark Richards
Mark Stevenson
Mark T Linn
Mark Waters
Martha Nicholson
Martin Hollywood
Martin Whelton
Martin Brampton
Martin Conneely
Mary Ann Horgan
Mary Bryan
Mary Morris
Mary Nash
Mary Wang
Mathias Enard

Matthew Francis
Matthew Shenton
Matthew Todd
Matthew Bates
Matthew Lawrence
Maureen Cooper
Maureen Freely
Maxime Dargaud-Fons
Melissa da Silveira
     Serpa
Michael Kitto
Michael & Christine
     Thompson
Michael Bagnall
Michael Harrison
Michael James
     Eastwood
Michael Johnston
Michael Thompson
Michelle Bailat-Jones
Michelle Purnell
Michelle Roberts
Miles Visman
Milo Waterfield
Minna Daum
Mirra Addenbrooke
Monika Olsen
Morgan Lyons
Moshi Moshi Records
Ms SA Harwood
Murali Menon

N Jabinh
Nadine El-Hadi
Nan Haberman
Nancy Scott

Naomi Frisby
Nasser Hashmi
Natalie Brandweiner
Natalie Rope
Natalie Smith
Natalie Wardle
Nia Emlyn-Jones
Nicholas Holmes
Nick Chapman
Nick Nelson &
    Rachel Eley
Nick Sidwell
Nicola Cowan
Nicola Hart
Nicola Ruffles
Nicolette Knoop
Nina Power
Nuala Grant
Nuala Watt

Octavia Lamb
Odhran Kelly
Oladele Olajide
Olga Zilberbourg
Omid Bagherli
Owen Booth

PD Evans
PM Goodman
Paddy Maynes
Pamela Ritchie
Pat Henwood
Patricia Appleyard
Patricia Melo
Patricia Hill
Patrick Coyne

Paul Cahalan
Paul Bailey
Paul Brand
Paul Dettman
Paul Gamble
Paul Hannon
Paul Jones
Paul Myatt
Paula Ruocco
Paulo Santos Pinto
Peter Rowland
Peter Law
Peter Lawton
Peter Murray
Peter Straus
Peter Vos
Phil Morgan
Philip Warren
Phyllis Reeve
Piet Van Bockstal
Polly McLean
Pria Doogan

Quentin Webb

Rachel Watkins
Rachel Henderson
Rachel Parkin
Rachel Pritchard
Rachel Van Riel
Rebecca Atkinson
Rebecca K Morrison
Rebecca Moss
Rebecca Rosenthal
Réjane Collard
Renata Larkin

Rhian Jones
Richard Carter &
    Rachel Guilbert
Richard Jackson
Richard Jacomb
Richard Martin
Richard Smith
Richard Soundy
Rishi Dastidar
Rob Fletcher
Robert & Clare
    Pearsall
Robert Delahunty
Robert Gillett
Robert Postlethwaite
Robin Patterson
Robin Woodburn
Ronnie Troughton
Ros Schwartz
Rose Alison Cowan
Rose Cole
Rose Skelton
Ross Macpherson
Ross Walker
Ruth Ahmedzai
Ruth Clarke
Ruth Fainlight
Ruth Mullineux
Ruth Stokes

Sabine Griffiths
Sally Baker
Sam Byers
Sam Ruddock
Samantha Sawers
Sandie Guine

Sandra de Monte
Sandra Hall
Sara D'Arcy
Sarah Butler
Sarah Bourne
Sarah Magill
Sarah Nicholls
Sarah Salway
Sarojini Arinayagam
Saskia Restorick
Scott Morris
Sean Malone
Sean McGivern
Seini O'Connor
Selin Kocagoz
Shan Osborne
Sharon Evans
Shazea Quraishi
Sheridan Marshall
Sherine El-sayed
Sian Christina
Sigrun Hodne
Simon Armstrong
Simon Okotie
Simon Blake
Simon M Garrett
Simon M Robertson
Simon Pare
Simon Petherick
Simon Wheeler
Sinead Fitzgerald
Sonia McLintock
Stefanie Freudenthal
Steph Morris
Stephanie Brada
Stephanie Ellyne

Stephen Walker
Stephen Abbott
Stephen Pearsall
Stewart MacDonald
Stewart McAbney
Stuart Condie
Sue Ritson
Sue & Ed Aldred
Sue Doyle
Sue Halpern
Susan Murray
Susan Tomaselli
Susan Bird
Susanna Jones
Susie Nicklin
Suzanne Smith
Suzanne Fortey
Suzanne Kirkham
Sylvie Zannier-Betts

Tamsin Ballard
Tania Hershman
Thomas Bell
Thomas Fritz
Tien Do
Tim Russ
Tim Theroux
Tim Warren
Tina Andrews
Tina Rotherham-
     Winqvist
Toby Aisbitt
Tom Heel
Tom Bowden
Tom Long
Tom Mandall

Tom Russell
Tony & Joy Molyneaux
Tony Crofts
Torna Russel-Hills
Tracey Martin
Trevor Wald
Trish Hollywood

Vanessa Garden
Vanessa Nolan
Vanessa Wells
Venetia Welby
Verena Weigert
Victoria Adams
Victoria O'Neill
Vinita Joseph
Viviane D'Souza
Vivien
     Doornekamp-Glass

Walter Prando
Wendy Knee
Wiebke Schwartz
Will Buck & Jo Luloff
William Black
William G Dennehy
William Prior
Winifred June
     Craddock

Yvonne Overell

Zoe Brasier
Zoë Laughton

Current & Upcoming Books by And Other Stories

Title: *All Dogs are Blue*
Author: Rodrigo de Souza Leão
Editors: Ana Fletcher & Sophie Lewis
Copy-editor: Wendy Toole
Proofreader: Alex Middleton
Typesetter: Tetragon
Set in: 11/15.5pt Swift Neue Pro, Verlag
Series and Cover Design: Joseph Harries
Format: B Format with French flaps
Paper: Munken Premium Cream 17.5 80gsm FSC
Printer: T J International Ltd, Padstow, Cornwall

FSC
www.fsc.org
MIX
Paper from
responsible sources
FSC® C013056